Scientist Werner Brecht had discovered a fantastically sophisticated alien spacecraft on the moon, and now every nation on Earth vied for the chance to possess its secrets . . .

"What's inside?" demanded the Premier of Common Europe.

"I suspect," Brecht said, "that inside the ship is information beyond our wildest dreams: their technology and science, presented in such a manner that we can decipher and utilize it."

President Rice was indignant. Why the hell did Brecht refuse to tell them where the craft was hidden, when so much depended upon it?

"Confound it, man," Rice said, "don't you see we've got to open that thing immediately? You owe it to the human race, to Earth, to reveal its location."

Brecht shook his head impatiently. "You see, the intelligent beings who sent that vessel to us made one very basic mistake: they assumed that before our technological culture was developed enough to send probes to the moon and discover their ship, we would have achieved civilization."

Everyone was staring at him now, his own international teammates as well as the distinguished visitors.

"But we haven't," he finished simply.

SPACE VISITOR

by
Mack Reynolds

WILDSIDE PRESS

SPACE VISITOR

Copyright © 1977 by Mack Reynolds

by Mack Reynolds:

CHAPTER ONE

FIVE OF THEM were seated about the central table of the recreation room. In name it was the recreation *hall,* but it just wasn't as big as all that. Bring up a dozen visiting firemen, plus the three-man crew of the spacecraft, and the place was packed. However, it was a reasonably charming room, made livable with paintings and other art, complete with comfortable furniture, a well-stocked bar, Tri-Di television, and of all things, a ping-pong table. Ping-pong took a bit of getting used to in these parts; for that matter, even a card game could take some getting used to.

They were, reading from left to right, Mary Lou Pickett, American; Kingsley Brett-James, Englishman; Max Zimmerman, Israeli; Li Ching, Chinese; and Azikiwe Awolowo, Nigerian. They spoke to each other in Esperanto, for policy reasons, though all knew English, and each of them liked each of the others as much as they had ever liked anyone. They had to; it was a matter of survival.

1

They were playing Liar's Dice, once-favorite of the Royal Air Force when the chips were down during the Battle of Britain.

Max Zimmerman shook the dice cup with a flourish, banged it down on the table and peered beneath the edge, hiding the cup from his neighbors with his other hand. Smiling broadly, he announced, "Three aces," and passed the cup to Li Ching.

She looked at him suspiciously. A wisp of a girl incongruously dressed in coveralls rather than in a cheongsam dress, her native costume which would have set off to perfection her slender figure, she murmured, "I don't trust you people, even if you swore on a stack of Talmuds, with one hand leaning up against the Wailing Wall."

"I am stung to the quick," Zimmerman protested. "We of Israel are noted for our honesty—especially when leaning on the Wailing Wall."

Brett-James took up the banter. The most stereotyped upper-class Britisher ever to come down the pike, he even had that slight flaring of the nostrils that would seem to indicate that at all times the others in his vicinity were lesser-breeds-without-the-law. He was somewhat slight of build, and drawled when he spoke, with an Eton accent that came through even in Esperanto.

He said, "Did you hear the one about the Jew who was rending his clothing and pounding his head against the Wailing Wall, crying, 'My people, my people, I want to return to my people.'? A tourist came along and listened for a while, then said finally, 'Look, here you are in Jerusalem, don't you know. At long last you have realized your dreams, old boy. What do you mean, you want to return to your people? On the bloody face of it, here you are.' And the Jew said, 'Yes, but my people are all in Miami Beach.' "

Nobody bothered to laugh.

Max Zimmerman said sourly, "Have you ever heard the one about the Englishman who was buggering the swan in the Thames Estuary?" When nobody responded he turned to Li Ching, "Come on, Chink, do you accept or not? We can't screw you flying."

"The trouble with you is that you try to carry idioms over into Esperanto. It doesn't work." She sighed. "I'm a fool to trust a kike, but I accept."

She peered under the cup rim, and snorted with self-disgust. Bringing forth two aces instead of the three Zimmerman had called, she put them to one side while he beamed lovingly at her.

She shook the remaining three dice in the cup and banged it down on the table, peered beneath and turned to the Nigerian girl next to her. "Three aces and two jacks." She pushed the cup and the two exposed aces over. "Your turn, Nigger."

Azikiwe Awolowo didn't even bother to take the cup. "I don't trust you Chinks any further than I could throw the Great Wall of China," she declared.

Zimmerman clasped his right hand over his heart. He was a big man, not excessively heavy, his features Germanic rather than Semitic, down to blue eyes and dirty blond hair. Less than handsome, his face looked as though it had seen some battering in its time. It was understood, although he never talked about it, that he had participated in some of the fracases with the Arabs as a younger man.

He said, "According to the Thoughts of Mao, a doubting woman is like hemorrhoids."

Kingsley Brett-James murmured, "Have any of you read that American writer's book, *A Connecticut Yankee in King Arthur's Hemorrhoids*? A homosexual novel, you know."

A couple of them bothered to groan.

"I do say, I thought it was we English who were supposed to have no sense of humor."

Azikiwe Awolowo said, "I challenge," and picked up the dice cup. There was no extra ace there and no pair of jacks.

Li Ching rolled her almond eyes upward. "I should have known better than to try and fool a nigger."

Max Zimmerman laughed and took up the score pad. "That makes you P-I, Chink. All you need is the G and you're P-I-G and have to buy the drinks." He thought for a moment. "Come to think of it, we better cut out the drinks. Make it a round of pot."

"Why?" Mary Lou protested. "I don't particularly like grass."

Zimmerman looked at her. "Because, Yawl, booze is a depressant. And we need depressants like another half a dozen holes in the head. As team doctor and psychiatrist, I'm of the opinion that a hangover can help lead to space cafard. So far on this tour of duty, we've escaped. Let's keep it that way."

"You're right," she agreed. It was her turn to

4

throw the dice, but she made no move to reach for the cup. Sighing, she said, "What in the world are we doing here?"

"Not in the world," Brett-James responded. "In Luna. And what we're doing is playing Liar's Dice, for want of anything more diverting."

"No, what I mean is, well, what are we doing sitting here?"

Azikiwe said reasonably, "We're sitting here because we've got lead in our pants. Otherwise, a slight movement and we'd be drifting around the room."

Zimmerman laughed. "Not lead in our pants. The damned things themselves are magnetized." He smiled at Mary Lou. "Listen, Yawl, you know perfectly well why we Lunatics are here. If we weren't, every time a bunch of these first-tripper scientists, technicians, or other visiting firemen came up to mess around with the Luna Radio Interferometer Observatory, they'd kill themselves off left and right. Can you imagine them getting into spacesuits on their own? Some of the attempts I've seen would chill your blood."

Mary Lou nodded. "Did you ever see one try to flush a toilet for the first time here in the Luna Hilton?"

"The dice, the dice, old girl," said Brett-James.

Mary Lou shook the dice box, banged it down on the table and peered beneath, her perfect teeth biting her lower lip. She wasn't a pretty woman by the usual standards, but she projected an undeniable beauty. Her hair was golden, though cropped short for practical reasons, but even the coveralls she wore, as did the others, couldn't

5

disguise her fine figure. A Southern accent slightly coated her Esperanto.

While she considered, Zimmerman asked, "Where's the Kraut?"

Mary Lou answered, "Werner's out in the Jaguar scouting around the moonscape. Four jacks . . ." She pushed the dice cup toward Brett-James. ". . . .There you are, Your Majesty."

The Englishman looked at her unbelievingly. "Four jacks! On the first roll? I say, do you expect me to believe that?"

Her expression was guileless.

Zimmerman shook his head, "Brecht is the only one on the team that ever bothers to go out on the surface when he doesn't have to. If it weren't for the fact that here we are on the moon, I'd diagnose him as moonstruck, possibly a werewolf. He's the only person in the history of the Observatory who's signed up for three tours of duty. When I first got here, I saw all I wanted to see of the surface of this godforsaken satellite in my first half hour."

Azikiwe was chuckling. Her complexion was as ebony as a Sengalese but, like so many Nigerians, she undoubtedly had a considerable number of Arab ancestors, the result being her features were almost Caucasian.

"What's funny?" Li Chang asked.

"I was thinking of our calling that gawky sand-dune buggy a Jaguar. While I was a student in England I drove a real Jaguar. It was a wonderful car."

Brett-James added, "But I'd hate to drive it up

6

here, don't you know." He turned to Mary Lou accusingly, "Yawl, you are a liar," and upped the dice box. There were the four jacks.

After marking the score card, Zimmerman announced, "Your Majesty, that makes you a P-I-G. It's your buy." He looked around. "Does anybody really want another joint?"

"Not me," said Mary Lou.

The others shook their heads. Ennui was obviously upon them.

"What was on the news today?" Zimmerman asked Brett-James. "I can't bring myself to listen to it any more; it's too grim."

"Why lay yourself open to ulcers, old chap?" the communications man responded. "The Soviet Complex and the People's Republic of China are still making spitting sounds. China refuses to join the Soviet Complex on the grounds that it's rightist-revisionist, whatever that is. United America and Common Europe are wrangling about the value of the pseudo-dollar again, and some elements in Europe are advocating that all American corporations there be nationalized to pay for all the funny-money that's been laid on them by the Yanks. Brazil and the Argentine have been snarling. Bolivia and Paraguay have lined up with Brazil; Uruguay and Chile with Argenta. Peru is on the sidelines. But this time it looks as though there might be a shooting war. That Mendoza crowd in Brazil wants to amalgamate the whole continent into a United States of South America. They figure it's the only way they can compete on the world scene. Thank God they don't have atomic weapons."

"Can't the Reunited Nations do something?" Azikiwe asked.

Brett-James smiled sadly at her. "All I can say to that is you are one naive nigger."

"Was there anything at all on the space cafard experiments?" asked Zimmerman.

The Englishman shook his head. "Not so far as a cure is concerned. They've got the causes nailed down to claustrophobia, fear of free fall, monotony—in short, sheer boredom and an instinctive fear of the blackness of space, particularly here on the dark side. But there are some other factors that baffle them. Thus far it would seem that man doesn't like to live out of his own backyard, as it were."

"Which reminds me," Li Ching put in. "Our tour of duty is up in a month and we haven't had a single case of cafard. Isn't that some sort of record? I wonder who will be in the next team. They must be getting near the end of their year's training."

Mary Lou said, "Two from the Soviet Complex—a Bulgarian and a Pole, one from Japan, one from India, one from New Zealand, and I think that the remaining one is an Argentine."

Zimmerman looked unhappy. "A Jap, eh? There have only been two Japs sent up here and both of them came down with space cafard in the first few weeks. It would seem that our sons of Nippon are patsies for space madness."

Li Ching yawned and turned to Zimmerman, "Why don't we go to bed, darling?"

"Brett-James shifted in his chair. "Max, old

8

boy, why don't you and I switch women for a spell?"

The Israeli answered solemnly, "I'd love to, Your Majesty, but the Chink here knows kempo and she's threatened to break my ass if I mess around with other women."

"Damn well told," Li Ching affirmed.

"I say, that would be a shame." Brett-James looked at the Nigerian. "Besides, Azikiwe is a whiz at judo, and she threatened to break both of my arms under the same circumstances. He turned to Mary Lou. "What are Yawl an expert at, a switch-blade?"

Mary Lou yawned too. "No, Your Majesty, but I've got an excellent left hook. I wonder where the Kraut is."

"I could get a fix on him if you wanted," the communications man offered. "He's wearing his electronic I.D. tag, I should imagine. For that matter, old thing, you could call him on the radio in the Jaguar."

"No, he doesn't like to be bothered when he's zipping around checking out the rocks. I think he figures on finding diamonds."

It was then that Werner Brecht entered. He walked almost as though he were Earthside. Three tours of duty on Luna spaced over a period of three years had accustomed him to the almost meaningless gravity to a degree probably never achieved by any other Earthling. It was difficult to believe he too depended upon magnetized shoes.

"Well, here's the Boche now," Brett-James said. "We were just discussing swapping bed

9

companions. I understand it's all the thing down in United America these days."

"Ha," Mary Lou snorted. "Once a lecherous limey, always a lecherous limey, begging your pardon, Your Majesty."

"By George, think nothing of it, Yawl," the Englishman said magnanimously.

Werner Brecht made a beeline for the small bar the recreation hall boasted. There were half a dozen bottles on it, all embedded in magnetic bases, as were the dozen or so glasses of various sizes. He picked up a bottle which had his name scrawled across the label in pencil and poured himself a tremendous slug of Scotch. Not bothering with ice, water, or mixer, he brought his drink to the table and slumped into a chair.

Zimmerman regarded the glass, then said gently, "Look, Kraut, up here we're supposedly rationed to a fifth of booze a week per person. Some of the double-domes think it causes a tendency to space cafard."

"Go obscenity thyself," Brecht said. "This is an emergency. Besides, I've been up here for three tours and I've never even been touched by cafard."

Brett-James interjected, "Or, screw you, Jack, I'm all right."

Brecht looked at him strangely. "Your Majesty, the bets are now down, and the world is going to be in the clutch."

"Darling, what's the matter?" Mary Lou asked in a bewildered voice.

Zimmerman was on his feet. "Werner! You don't feel any symptoms of cafard, do you?"

10

Brecht regarded him solemnly. "No, it's not that. I'm not even sure I want to tell you, but I suppose I have to." He took a gulp of his drink.

"Darling . . ." Mary Lou began.

He turned to her. "Listen, Yawl. I've found an extraterrestrial spaceship."

CHAPTER TWO

UNDOUBTEDLY, IT HAD all started as far back as 1931 when Karl G. Jansky of the Bell Telephone Laboratories was exploring radio-frequency disturbances in the atmosphere. He came to the conclusion that, although local and distant thunderstorms were responsible for most disturbances, there was a third noise-component which could only be extraterrestrial in origin.

Another American, Grote Reber, was fascinated by Jansky's discoveries. He went on to construct the first radio telescope with a dish antenna thirty-one feet in diameter.

It was a good beginning. However, as human knowledge was doubling every eight years, by 1960 the U.S. Department of Defense began construction on a one-thousand-foot reflector to conduct ionospheric research. The site was a natural depression in the earth at Arecibo, in Puerto Rico. The Lebedev Institute of Moscow, with its Leningrad and Crimean observatories, was also getting into the act; and so were the British, French, Dutch, and Australians.

Meanwhile, breakthroughs in other areas were taking place. In 1943, Astronomer Peter Van de Kamp discovered some small irregularities in the double-star system 61 Cygni, indicating that a third component, evidently non-luminous, must exist. A planet, he pondered? If so, then it must be some eight times the mass of Jupiter.

In 1960, they turned up another planet, roughly the same size, circling the small star Lalande 21185. And in 1963, Barnard's Star, only six light years from Earth, also indicated a planet, this one only about one and a half times the mass of Jupiter.

Barnard's Star is second closest to earth, Lalande 21185 third, and 61 Cygni twelfth. A switch in scientific thinking occurred: the solar system is not unique; other stars, if not most, also have planetary systems; and if they have planets the size of Jupiter and larger, then they very well might have smaller ones the size of Earth, perhaps too small to detect with present-day equipment.

Excitement sped through scientific circles. Other planets—possibly other life? *Intelligent life?*

The search was on.

Then, in 1973, articles by Duncan A. Lunan appeared in *Spaceflight*, the publication of the British Interplanetary Society, and *Analog*, a popular American magazine, that electrified the world. The author claimed to have translated a message that had possibly been relayed to earth by robot spacecraft from an advanced culture far beyond the solar system. He was of the opinion that the automatic spacecraft might have been circling the moon for thousands of years, waiting for Earth to progress to the point where it would be able to respond to the message.

Our home is Epsilon Bootis, which is a double star. We live on the sixth planet of seven—check that, the sixth of seven— counting outward from the sun, which is the larger of the two stars. Our sixth planet has one moon. Our fourth planet has three. Our first and third planets each have one. Our probe is in the orbit of your moon.

Lunan's theory began with an experiment conducted by the Norwegian geophysicist Carl Stormer and a Dutch colleague, Balthasar van der Pol. Sending each other a number of short-wave radio messages, they discovered a strange side effect: at times the messages were followed by mysterious echoes that were picked up as many as fifteen seconds after the original transmission. It was in 1960 that radio astonomer Ronald Bracewell came up with a possible explanation of the echoes mystery. In an article for *Nature*, he speculated that an advanced civilization that wanted to communicate with others might not use long-range radio signals because such signals would weaken over interstellar distance. Instead, he postulated, they might use robot spacecraft as message bearers. Sent to the vicinity of a promising nearby star, the probe could swing into orbit at about the right distance to encounter a planet with life-supporting temperatures. If it picked up telltale radio signals, the probe might bounce them back to advertise its presence, thereby producing the mysterious echoes of the 1920s.

Fascinated by Bracewell's article, Lunan had got hold of the original reports made by Carl Stormer. Suspecting a code, he attempted to graph the echoes. One axis was a measure of the amount of time each echo was delayed. The other axis indicated the position of each echo in the sequence. Then he reversed the axes, and the result was striking: a collection of dots that looked to him like a sky map of the constellation Bootis, with the double star Epsilon Bootis significantly out of place. Lunan explained that might be the starship's way of saying that Epsilon Bootis was its place of origin.

Further research indicated that Arcturus, the constellation's brightest star, was situated in the suggested map in roughly the position it had occupied thirteen thousand years ago. Lunan's theory was that that dated the time the probe arrived in the Earth's vicinity and instructed its computerized equipment to scan the skies and draw up the star map.

Immediately, others began to send off blip-like radio signals into space at regular thirty-second intervals in hopes of stirring the space probe into another response.

At approximately the same time, the United States sent off the first message-bearing spacecrafts, Pioneer Ten and Pioneer Eleven, aimed to pass near enough to Jupiter to send back pictures and data, make a half turn about the giant planet, and then soar out into space. Both were equipped with a message to any alien civilization which might some day intercept it. Each of the Pioneers carried plaques showing two nude human figures, with other information in symbols that NASA hoped were universal. Maps of the solar system and the planet Earth were also included.

It was shortly after that the Glormar Explorer of the Hughes Tool Company began the controversial mining of the deep-sea beds for manganese nodules, billions of tons of which were estimated to be on the ocean floor. Some parts of the Pacific floor were literally paved with potato-sized nodules rich in manganese, copper, nickel, and cobalt.

Immediately delegates from ninety-one nations met in Geneva to wrangle over the jurisdiction of the international deep-sea beds. A hectic international scramble to grab this wealth of priceless resources developed. It was finally resolved that twenty-five percent of all profits taken from the ocean's beds would go to the new Reunited Nations, to be utilized for the human race as a whole. Otherwise, the ocean's bottom was available to all to exploit.

It was not surprising that the first truly major effort of the Reunited Nations was the creation of an ultra-large radio telescope on the far side of the moon, to search space for fellow intelligent life. Thousands of automated shuttlecraft hoisted men and materials to orbiting spaceships, which in turn ferried them over to Luna. Hundreds of technicians were trained to assemble three gigantic antenna dishes each a mile across. They were nestled in separate craters but connected to a single receiver.

The observatory was under remote control from Earth by the Ozma Department of the Reunited Nations, the name derived from Project Ozma, which, under the leadership of Frank D. Drake, had been the first to attempt to listen in on potential extraterrestrial radio emanations. After two months of negative results, the project was suspended, but by no means had the dream been given up.

To avoid meteorites, Luna City, or what some were want to call the Luna Hilton, was constructed beneath the moon's surface. It housed a permanent group of six: two communications technicians, one doctor-psychiatrist, one geologist, one chief-cook-and-bottle-washer, and one so-called recreation officer. Their principle task was to take care of visitors from earth, many of whom were in space for the first time. Their tour of duty lasted six months, the pensions they then received were fabulous; and none, with one exception, ever volunteered for a second tour of duty. Prolonged stay on Luna, no matter what the pay, was universally undesirable.

The one exception, Werner Brecht, was now seated in the recreation hall of the Luna Hilton, his five companions gaping at him, his own expression defensive.

Max Zimmerman said anxiously, "Jesus Christ,

Kraut, are you out of your ever-lovin' mind? What do you mean you've found an extraterrestrial spaceship?''

Brecht sighed. From a pocket of his coveralls he brought forth a small sheaf of Poloroid-type photos and tossed them to the table, then knocked back the balance of his drink.

"There you are," he said gratuitously.

The other five had already gathered around.

Brett-James exclaimed, "I say, by George, it looks like one of those early Russian Vostoks such as the one Yuri Gagarin used. Possibly somehow it crashed and——'' He let the sentence dribble away.

Brecht shook his head. "No dice, Your Majesty." He hunted around in the photos for one that depicted him standing next to the mysterious spacecraft, slightly under a rock ledge. He said, "I put the camera on a tripod and self-timed it to get this shot. The thing's twice the size of a Vostok, and it doesn't look like any other spacecraft ever manufactured on Earth, either."

They were still gawking, still unbelieving.

He said, "There's something else." He fished into another pocket and came up with a potato-sized rock. "I took this from underneath it."

It was absolutely quiet in the recreation hall. None of them knew what he was building up to.

He said very slowly, "I'll have to check further, in the lab, but unless I'm very much mistaken, this rock is older than that period in which life first was formed in the oceans of our world."

"Wow!" Azikiwe let out finally. "Let's get into our spacesuits and go out and see it."

"Bloody right," Brett-James exclaimed, turning in the direction of the room which housed the nearest spacelock.

"Wait a minute," Brecht said quietly. He got up and headed to the bar and poured himself another stiff Scotch, once again ignoring ice or mix.

They all looked at him, waiting.

"I'm not taking you to it."

CHAPTER THREE

ZIMMERMAN STARED AT him as though the other were demented. "What in the hell are you talking about? It's the biggest discovery in the history of the human race: We are not alone in the galaxy."

"That's what I'm talking about," Brecht said doggedly, knocking back half of the second drink. "Frankly, I'm afraid."

"Afraid?" Mary Lou echoed. "Afraid of what, darling?"

"Not of what," he told her. "For whom. I'm afraid for the human race."

He returned to his chair and slumped into it. One by one, the others went to the bar and poured drinks for themselves before coming back to the table.

Brecht was a small man, Latin in appearance in spite of his name. His hair was dark and so were his eyes, his teeth sparkling white when he smiled, which wasn't often. He was small and wiry and moved with a quick grace. He had few friends but among them where these five, for any one of whom he would have given his life; only partially because back on earth, before taking this most recent Luna tour of duty, the psychiatrists of the Ozma Department had implanted that affection hypnotically.

He said now, weariness in his voice, "I discovered the damn thing on my first tour here, three years ago. My first inclination was to reveal it immediately, of course, and go down in history as the first man to discover an extraterrestrial artifact. But then I had second thoughts.

"This alien life form had reached a level of technology that enabled them to cross space . . . possibly before the lowest life form had even begun to evolve on earth. . . ."

"I say, old chap, what's that got to do with it?" Brett-James asked.

Brecht eyed him. "Don't you see? Sooner or later we are going to come up against this intelligence. Do you know what, Your Majesty? The human race is crazy as bedbugs."

Brett-James murmured, "You're not making much sense, Kraut."

"Maybe he is," Mary Lou said thoughtfully. "Go on, Werner."

He took a deep breath. "Let's face it, an intelligent life form can't develop technologically without at the same time developing ethical and moral codes along with it. Why? Because eventually it reaches the point where the culture will destroy itself without such codes. We reached that point—the ability to destroy ourselves—with the advent of nuclear weapons. The United States, which first developed the A-bomb, didn't have a moral code strong enough to keep it from destroying two Japanese cities, even though Japan was already reeling, and the better part of the world was zeroing in on her by that time since the threat of Germany and Italy had been eliminated. Within a few years, the Soviet Union had nuclear fission bombs, and even beat the Americans to the ones based on fusion. The British, French, and Chinese did not lag far behind——"

"The People's Republic was forced to develop them in self-defense," Li Ching interrupted.

The geologist didn't bother to respond. He went on, "The world went into an unprecedented arms race. Hundreds of billions were spent to develop ever more powerful bombs and more efficient missiles with which to deliver or intercept them. And when man went into space it was with full competition between nations, not cooperation. Today, any of the great powers, Common Europe, United America, the Soviet Complex, the People's Republic of China, could destroy that whole planet of ours several times over. And they're all ready to do it, given any kind of a slip."

He paused to look around at each of them, then shook his head.

"With this mentality, are we ready to contact alien life forms undoubtedly far, far more advanced than we are in science?"

Zimmerman shifted unhappily in his chair. "That's all very well, but the thing's there and we can't make it go away by ignoring it. We've got to find out why it's there, where it came from, and how it managed to get across deep space."

"Jolly well told," Brett-James agreed somewhat indignantly.

Brecht grunted. "Have you ever considered why we are sitting here at the Luna Radio Interferometer Observatory patiently directing our radio telescope all about this area of the galaxy, listening for intelligent communications attempts, but at the same time not directing our own signals into space for other intelligences to pick up?"

They scowled at him uncomprehendingly.

"The reason is the Ozma Department wants to know where *they* are, but they are afraid to let them know where *we* are. We're still seeing it in terms of bug-eyed monsters, or little green men with death rays who want to conquer the Earth. I'm not going to reveal the location of that starship until I know what the world is going to do about it."

Azikiwe took up the photos again and looked through them carefully. "I note that you've fuzzed out the background by focusing with very little depth. There's no hint in the pictures of their location."

"It won't wash," Brett-James said. "We'll go out with metal detectors. There are several of them, top strength, in the engineer's warehouse."

Brecht shook his head. "No dice. Remember, I've been checking out the thing for three tours of duty. I don't think it's made of metal, not as we know it. Neither the hull, nor anything inside reacts to a metal detector."

Mary Lou asked, "You couldn't hear anything, I suppose?"

He shook his head. "Not even with a gimmick

the engineers call an electronic-stethoscope which will theoretically pick up a mouse's footsteps across a table through a couple of inches of steel."

They searched for sensible questions, still not quite able to accept what he was telling them.

Zimmerman asked, "What else did you do?"

"I checked out the hull with everything I could think of—acids, a diamond drill, so on and so forth." He shrugged. "I couldn't even scratch it with the drill and none of my chemicals reacted to it."

"Heavens to Betsy!" Mary Lou exclaimed.

"Was there any kind of an entry?" asked Li Ching.

"Something that could have been one. Circular, similar to a porthole. Too small for an ordinary man, but a child, or possibly a small woman such as you, Chink, could make it."

Zimmerman asked the next question: "Did you try to open it?"

"I considered it but decided that it better wait until such experts as we can dream up are present. Or possibly it should be shipped back to Earth where it can be worked on under laboratory conditions. I don't know, but I didn't want to open Pandora's box, so to speak."

"It still won't wash, Kraut." Zimmerman was emphatic. "It's there. We've got to reveal its existence. When we report it—report you've found it—they'll send up a few dozen technicians and they'll find it sooner or later."

Brecht shook his head. "Oh no they won't. If you'll check the Jaguar, you'll find a pickax and a crowbar. I jimmied that rock ledge down and buried the spacecraft.''

Brett-James raised his eyes upwards in a gesture of despair. He picked up two of the best photos, including the one with Brecht in it, and said, "Come on, Chink."

Li Ching blinked. "Where?"

"To the communications room. It's time we checked in with the Ozma Department. Who the hell's the director this month, that Swede? You'd better come too, Kraut. He'll probably bust your eardrums at the other end of the 230,000 miles involved. They say he's got a temper like a male walrus in breeding season."

"We'll all come," Zimmerman said, standing.

They filed down the hall to the communications room. Brett-James took his place behind the Rube Goldberg board and screen; Li Ching, his second in command, stood behind hers, almost an exact duplicate. Communications officers were duplicated on the Luna teams in case one of them came down with space cafard. Anybody else was more or less expendable, but they had to have communication with the home planet.

The others stood around and watched.

Finally the last switch was flicked, a last dial twisted. "Luna City calling Ozma Department. Brett-James here. Come in, Ozma."

The laser-beam he was utilizing bounced off the small communications satellite stationed permanently above the Observatory and took off on its way to Mother Earth. The communications officer, and everyone else in the room, waited out the two-and-a-half-second time lag each way.

A face faded onto the screen, a sleepy-looking face. "Ozma Department. Harlan Jones here. Hi, Kingsley, what's up?"

"I want to have a scrambled talk with Director Nilsson Vogel. I mean, really scrambled, Harlan. Not even you."

"Are you completely around the bend, Kingsley? It's two o'clock here in Greater Washington."

"I dare say. However it is D-Day here. Get him on soonest, Harlan. This is top-top emergency."

"See what I can do."

Ten minutes passed.

A new face faded onto the screen, irritated, a heavy Scandinavian face more than averagely wrinkled for a man in his early sixties. He glared at Brett-James and rumbled, "Well?"

The Englishman asked, "Is this scrambled, sir?"

"So Harlan Jones tells me."

"Sir, Werner Brecht, our team geologist, has discovered an extraterrestrial spacecraft in seemingly perfect condition."

The number of seconds that passed before the reply came could not be attributed solely to the time lag.

The face on the screen was incredulous. "Are you down with space cafard, Brett-James? Immediately repeat what you just said in detail."

"Yes, sir. Exploring with one of the Luna vehicles, geologist Werner Brecht has discovered an extraterrestrial spacecraft." Brett-James put the two photos against the screen. "Here are pictures of it."

The Director muttered something in Swedish

that sounded like heartfelt profanity, then said in Esperanto, "Put him on immediately."

Werner Brecht slid into the chair Brett-James vacated for him, before the screen. The Englishman stood to one side, watching the controls, delicately adjusting a dial here and there at intervals.

Brecht said slowly, "I discovered the space vehicle on my first tour of duty. Since than I have been examining it to the best of my ability. I'll have to wait until I have Earthside access to laboratories and am in a position to confer with colleagues more advanced in the field than myself before I am certain, but I believe the vehicle has been on Luna for millions of years."

"Good God! Is it intact?"

"Yes, as Commander Brett-James reported, it is seemingly in perfect condition. It was under an outcropping of rock, quite secure from small meteorites at least."

"I'll have a team of appropriate technicians up there within days. Don't touch it meanwhile. How far from Luna City is it located?"

Werner Brecht looked directly into his superior's eyes. "I won't tell you that, sir."

CHAPTER FOUR

THEY WENT BY THE twenty-four-hour clock and adhered to their schedule religiously. Meals and sleeping hours were always the same, be it age-long night or age-long day. It was the only possible way to keep their physical and mental health intact. In his insistence on routine, Max Zimmerman was almost tyrannical.

It wasn't long after the call to the director of the Ozma Department on Earth that Zimmerman and Li Ching entered their quarters.

Theoretically, there was no official position on the sleeping arrangements of the staff of the Radio Interferometer Observatory. However, six months on the surface of the moon was bad enough; not having normal sexual relations, in addition to all other discomforts, would have been an unnecessary hardship. In practice, therefore, it was a bit of a setup. The teams always consisted of three men and three women, all between the ages of thirty and forty, all free of close entanglements,

28

including marriage, at home. They were screened out for racial or nationalistic prejudices, and homosexuality. Thus it was that the Ozma Department not only allowed such relationships but actually encouraged them, though this was a little-known fact among the average citizens back on Earth. Too many howls might have gone up on the part of religious groups and other puritanical elements.

From time to time, minor staff difficulties popped up due to the pairing off, but on the average, the persons mutually selected remained together for the whole six months. There was another very good reason for the lack of conflicts in general: their training included an hypnotically induced suggestion that made them unable to dislike, or in any manner wish ill of, any of the others on the team.

Max Zimmerman and Li Ching undressed and prepared for bed in thoughtful silence. Their quarters were far from Spartan. Every effort had been made to equip the Luna Hilton with all the Earth comforts. The very low gravity took some getting used to, of course, but otherwise one could have imagined oneself in a small hotel suite back home.

Usually they would have made love at this point, but tonight there were other things on their minds.

"Max, there are some very frightening aspects to all this. The more I think about them, the more frightening they become."

"I know," he said, putting an arm about her shoulders and bringing the warmth of her body to him. "What in particular are you thinking about?

29

I've dreamed up some frightening aspects of my own."

"If that thing has been there for millions of years, by this time how much further advanced is this other intelligent life form? They were already further along than we are now when they made it. What are they by now, Max—gods?"

"Probably," he muttered. But then, "Of course, there's always the possibility that they are no longer in existence."

"How could that be?" she asked, puzzled.

"Perhaps something has happened to them. Perhaps the sun system in which they originated went into nova. Perhaps they were wiped out in an interplanetary or even interstellar conflict, though that would seem unlikely. Perhaps they destroyed themselves in a war, as we threaten to do here on Earth. Perhaps a lot of things. Perhaps they became bored and committed suicide."

"Max, don't be ridiculous."

He looked at her without smiling. "It's not impossible, you know. Our own race is now on the verge of attaining immortality, due to the rate of medical and biological breakthroughs. Suppose we do achieve it. Do you, for instance, want immortality, Li Ching?"

"Why, I've never even thought about it, but . . . of course. It would be great to live for an indefinite time, instead of the hundred or so years we can figure on now."

He frowned before saying doubtfully, "I don't know. I guess that the first thousand years would be the easiest."

"Thousand years?" she repeated blankly.

"Yes, of course: immortality. After about ten thousand years, don't you think you might experience a little weariness?"

She thought about it for a moment but then shook her head. "No. If the race was as advanced as all that, they would devise some method of maintaining the desire to live, find some great purpose to keep you going."

"Possibly," he said. "But the fact of the matter is, Li Ching, that life is an accident. It has no purpose."

"That's rather cynical, isn't it? It doesn't sound like you, Max."

"I wasn't trying to be cynical, simply realistic. Take our life form, mankind. One day, the sun will cool and life as we know it will be impossible in the solar system."

"Perhaps by that time we will have the know-how to move to other sun systems."

"Perhaps," he admitted. "But one day the galaxy itself will cool, or in some other manner cease to exist as a place where life can continue."

"Maybe by then the race will be so unbelievably advanced that we will be able to travel to other galaxies."

"Maybe. But some day, Li Ching, the universe itself will stop. . . . No, there is no purpose in life. A million years ago, an apeman was probably walking along a jungle path in what is now South Africa when a large predatory cat came along and killed and ate him. What was the purpose in his ever having lived? To breed and to become my ancestor? A million years from now, I will not be remembered as an individual any more than you and I remember that apeman. What's the purpose in my living?''

''I don't know,'' she said softly. ''It seems so worthless, the way you put it.''

''In the long run, it *is* worthless. I suppose I'm a hedonist: eat, drink, and be merry for tomorrow we kick off. The only thing that makes sense is to live it up while you are here, have as good a time as you can.''

He lay there for a long time without speaking, then turned his head.

Li Ching was asleep. He gently removed his arm from about her and turned over. Just before he fell asleep, he wondered why, if the other life form was able to send a space probe to Luna a million years and more ago, it had never sent another one.

Not surprisingly, in their own quarters Werner Brecht and Mary Lou Pickett had touched on some of the same aspects of the question.

As opposed to Max and Li Ching, however, they had made love first, to relax the tensions that had built up so strongly the past few hours. Now both lay staring up at the ceiling.

Mary Lou said finally, ''Werner, is it necessary that this extraterrestrial life form be far more advanced than we are in the sciences?''

He frowned. ''How could they be otherwise if they were able to build a spaceship that could travel light years in distance? It's all we can do now to explore the nearer planets in our own solar system.''

''Yes, I know, but . . . well, man is a rapidly

developing race—especially this past century. Couldn't they be a very slowly developing life form? That is, perhaps it took them millions of years to get to the point where they could get into space. But look how fast we go: less than seventy-five years after the Wright Brothers made that first flight of theirs at Kitty Hawk, we were on the moon. Orville Wright actually lived to see first spacecraft, the German V-2."

"You think that possibly they have the equivalent of a lower I.Q. than we boast, eh?"

"Why not, darling? Suppose you had a life form with an average I.Q. of fifty say, or even less, as opposed to the average human I.Q. of a hundred. Given time, lots of time, wouldn't they slowly evolve to the point where they would have the technology to build spaceships?"

"No, I don't think so. This isn't my field, of course, but I don't believe that's the way it works. You see, that old story about insects—ants, termites, cockroaches, or whatever—someday evolving and taking over the world is nonsense."

"Why?"

"Because," he told her, "you need three things in order to develop a culture of science and advanced technology. To begin with, you've got to have an animal, or other being, that has a fairly good brain. It has to have a hand with an opposed thumb . . . or the equivalent. Then it's got to have a voice box, or the equivalent, so that it can communicate its knowledge to its fellows and, more importantly, to its children. There's precious little value in accumulating knowledge in one generation if it can't be passed on to the next."

He paused to think it out some more, then went on: "For instance, according to studies the porpoise has at least as good a brain as has man, and it also has a voice box. But it hasn't got the hand. Hence no technology is possible for them.

"Then you have various Earthside life forms with a pretty good hand: the parrot, for example, which also has a voice box, but it has a birdbrain. Some of the apes, like man, do fairly well with all three but man copped a march on the rest of them and they never got off the ground."

Mary Lou said, "I don't see what this has to do with why a low I.Q. life form wouldn't, over a long period of time, develop scientifically and technologically."

"Well, as I understand it, you take some ape, a little smarter than the rest of them, with possibly a somewhat better voice box and a somewhat better hand. Okay, sooner or later he stumbles on some very primitive tools: a sharp flint rock, a stick which can be used as a club or to knock fruit out of a tree. His I.Q. is pretty damn low but it's high enough to use these new implements. Hell, even a chimp uses very simple tools. Those among the apemen who are smartest can use the tools best. Those who are strongest can clobber the other males best, and hence get the best females. Those who have the best voice boxes can communicate with their fellow apemen the best.

"Natural selection steps in over the millennia. The more stupid, the weakest, and those with inadequate voice boxes fall by the wayside. The original apeman who was our ancestor was probably no bigger than a chimpanzee, and not much

34

smarter, and probably didn't have any greater speaking ability—a chimp can be taught at least a couple of dozen words, you know. But over the millennia they slowly upgraded themselves. Within the period that scientists can study fairly accurately, we saw Cro-Magnon man take over from the Neanderthal, who didn't have quite enough on the ball.

"The process continued, and it is still going on. Those with the highest I.Q.s and in the best physical condition have the advantage in our society and automatically they get the best mates to breed with. Those with the lowest I.Q.s and in the worst physical condition very possibly don't breed at all. Those in between used to do the most breeding until the advent, recently, of population control. But even so, those top intelligence and physical specimens dominated the race, its science and its technology. And every generation that went by, its I.Q. and its physical well being grew."

Mary Lou said, "I'm beginning to see what you mean."

"The same would have to apply to any other advanced life form from the stars. They might start off with that I.Q. of fifty, but as they developed it would grow, along with the other attributes I mentioned. They might not even communicate by voice. They might have telepathy, or something we can't even conceive of. But communicate they must, and efficiently. They might not have a hand with an opposed thumb, but they would have the equivalent, something which could handle extremely delicate tools. That's the reason ants and cockroaches are out: no hand, no big brain; whether or not they can communicate anything complicated is irrelevant, never having accumulated it.''

He shook his head and ran his right hand over her belly. She closed her eyes in pleasure.

He said, "No. I'm afraid that this culture that was able to send a space probe across the void so long ago is millions of years ahead of our own species. God help us. . . .''

And then, for the first time since their lovemaking a while ago, he drove the subject from his mind.

Kingsley Brett-James was having at it from a different angle.

He said to his bed companion, who presented a startling picture of blackest ebony on white bedclothes, "I don't know what Werner has in mind and I suspect he doesn't either. He's playing it by ear. But if anything will stir up the international mess again since that bastard Hitler, this will be it.''

Azikiwe said, her voice unhappy, "Why not just throw it in the lap of the Reunited Nations? Let them open up the cursed thing and reveal the contents to everybody at once.''

"My dear girl, nobody would stand for it, I should think. Those countries with the greatest number of scientists, the greatest number of computers, the greatest amount of money and resources would dash into competition and the devil take the hindmost. Where would your Nigeria be while the Soviet Complex, United America, Common Europe, and even the People's Republic of China were wrenching the secrets of the stars from the extraterrestrial space probe? And the first of those four who came up with some ultra-weapon, or something that could be turned into one, would clobber the others immediately—before they discovered it too."

"I'm afraid you're right," she muttered even more unhappily.

CHAPTER FIVE

THEY WERE RELIEVED immediately. Or, rather, as
soon as the time it took to get a spacecraft up
from Earth. While they waited, all communications with the home planet were ordered scrambled and went directly to Nilsson Vogel, Director
of the Ozma Department, and to no one else. On
the face of it he was keeping the whole matter
under wraps, at least for the time being. They
debated what he had in mind among themselves,
but came up with a blank. They hadn't the
vaguest idea what he was going to do.

Supposedly, their tour of duty was to have
lasted another month. But that wasn't the way the
ball bounced. A second team was flown up from
Earth to take over.

Ordinarily, it was the practice for the team
being relieved to remain for a period of a couple
of weeks to break in the new group. Although all
volunteers for the Luna Radio Interferometer Observatory were given a full year of preliminary

instruction and training before their tour of duty, actually few had ever been in space before, or had been on short jaunts, perhaps shuttling to one of the orbiting space platforms. So it was considered best to orientate them.

This time, however, the Director of the Ozma Department obviously did not want to risk Brecht's team's dropping the information about the extraterrestrial craft to the newcomers. Strict orders came through that they were not even to talk with the new team; in fact, they were not even to see them.

In the strongest possible terms, Brecht and the others were also warned not to communicate whatsoever with the three-man crew of the spaceship that returned them to Earth. Even had they wished to do so, it was obvious that the spacemen, though mystified by the instructions, had been ordered not to speak to the team. Complete silence was maintained between the two groups all the way to the Earthside spaceport. A bit on the ridiculous side, considering the cramped quarters.

The team spent most of its time playing chess, cards, or reading. Largely, they were even silent among themselves, in spite of their affection for each other. There was a certain air of apprehensiveness about what was to come.

They had good reason to be glum.

Received at the spaceport near Greater Washington by a delegation of grim-looking Reunited Nations personnel, they were quickly bundled into a limousine, without being given the opportunity to speak to any of the numerous news media people who had gathered to interview the Luna crew which had returned prematurely from their tour of duty. Another limousine preceded them, sirens wailing, and one more followed.

Exactly one sentence was spoken to them by the burly type seated in front with the chauffeur. He said, very coldly, "You are ordered not to communicate with either myself or the chauffeur.".

"Get screwed, don't you know," Brett-James muttered. "I say, what in the world goes on here? I am a subject of His Majesty and object to this cavalier treatment."

The other promptly touched a button and a heavy panel of glass rolled up to seal off the driver's compartment from the rear, where they all sat.

"They're all heeled," said Zimmerman.

Azikiwe looked at him. "What do you mean, Kike?"

"They're all carrying guns. I thought the Reunited Nations was dedicated to peace."

"We'll see how much peace there'll be when this manure hits the fan, I should think," said the Englishman.

They were whisked to the Reunited Nations Building on the banks of the Potomac. All of them had been here before; the Ozma Department had its main headquarters in the building.

Zimmerman shook his head. "Can you feel this gravity? I'm glad we did our exercises as religiously as we did. Otherwise, we'd be on the floor of this car."

"I thought that we were supposed to go through

a week of rehabilitation, or whatever they call it, at the spaceport, before we were considered capable of normal activity," said Mary Lou.

"That was in the good old days," Brecht muttered. He had spoken little ever since they'd made their report to Director Vogel. He wasn't even particularly responsive to Mary Lou, who from time to time looked at him worriedly. He had also lost weight in spite of Zimmerman's urging that he eat better.

They pulled up before a side entrance of the massive building. The front car, its siren dying away for the first time since they'd left the spaceport, disgorged its half-dozen occupants who immediately assumed defensive positions around the limousine carrying the Luna team. The last of the three cars was also rapidly emptied. Four of the newcomers assumed positions on either side of the door, the two others entering the building, hands under their coats near their left armpits.

"I don't believe it," Mary Lou muttered.

"Bloody well better," Brett-James said in English. "You'd think we were VIPs."

Their guide, or bodyguard, opened the front door of the car, got out, looked up and down the street suspiciously, then opened the rear door and gestured for them to follow.

They filed out of the car, crossed the pavement, and entered the building. Their guards assumed positions all about them. The two who had gone in first had evidently cleared the hall: it was silent and empty. Across marble floors, they made their way to an elevator bank. Four of the men, including the chief guide, crowded into one car with the team, the others hurrying quickly to another elevator.

The door slid shut. "Penthouse," the guide said into the elevator's instruction screen.

Brett-James squirmed. All his instincts were to say something, some witty crack to ease the tension, but he couldn't bring himself to do it. Their bodyguards were so sincerely grim about the whole thing.

A surprisingly short time later the elevator reached the highest levels of the building; it must have been an express car to the penthouse only. They issued forth into a luxurious hallway.

Their four guards had exited first, hands beneath their coats. The second elevator arrived and the others got out.

The head man gestured commandingly and two of the bodyguards hurried off. Finally, they returned and nodded. It was safe to proceed.

The Luna team was marched into a small reception room. The door was closed behind them. They could hear the click of a lock.

The furniture was ornate, almost to the point of bad taste. The rug was the thickest any of them had ever walked on. Behind a large desk sat a man about thirty. He looked French.

He was very handsome, every feature all but perfect; the type of attractiveness that irritates many men and doesn't thrill as many women as is often assumed. He came to his feet at their entry and said, in a nice voice that went along with his face, "My name is Jean Hippolyte Foucault, and I am literally yours to command. I will live here with you, at least for the time being. I am in on the secret. I am a Moroccan of French descent, which is probably one of the reasons Director Vogel chose me. My nation is unaligned and has no particular interest in any of the ramifications of space travel.''

"What secret?'' Brecht asked bluntly.

The French-Moroccan smiled at him. "You are *Señor* Brecht?'' He used the Spanish form of address, rather than the Esperanto in which they were talking.

"That's right,'' Brecht said.

"The secret that a space probe, or whatever you wish to call it, has been found on Luna. A spacecraft from an intelligence alien to Earth. I don't believe it, of course, but that's the secret.''

"Would it be possible for us to go somewhere where we could sit down?'' Li Ching asked. "The gravity is terrible. I can hardly stand.''

Jean Foucault was immediately concerned. "Right this way,'' he said, ushering them through a door to the left of the desk.

In a monstrous living room that easily could have seated thirty persons on its collection of out-sized chairs and couches, the six of them slumped with undisguised relief into seats near each other.

Foucault was saying, "I am to be a cross between a butler, a bodyguard, an anti-press agent, a Man Friday, a bartender, and——''

"I say, what's a bloody anti-press agent?'' Brett-James interrupted.

The French-Moroccan looked at the Englishman. "Someone who keeps the press away. It is to be assumed they will make aggressive attempts to speak with you. The secret is already out—"

"It is?" Brecht exclaimed.

The other turned to him with his inevitable smile. "I was about to say that the secret is out that there is a secret. It's already known that something at least passingly strange has happened at the Ozma project. The rumors are that at long last you have picked up radio signals from space of an intelligent nature, which is why you've been hurried back to report before your six months were up. At any rate, in my role as bartender, could I get any of you a drink?"

"Jesus, yes," Zimmerman said, and the rest of them nodded.

There was an enormous and quite elaborately stocked bar against one wall of the living room. As Foucault crossed to it, he said over his shoulder, "Name your poison, as the Americans say. We have, or can order for you, literally anything. This penthouse, as you may possibly have guessed, usually houses the most important VIPs. I believe that last occupant was the Chairman of the Presidium from Moscow; in other words, Number One. Shall we say champagne?"

"By all means say it," Brett-James agreed. "And bring it."

"From the sizable refrigerator behind the bar, their Man Friday brought forth a magnum of champagne. He looked at the label critically. "Mumm's Cordon Rose, the very best of the celebrated pinks. Good vintage year, too."

As he was opening and pouring the wine, Brecht asked, "What was it you said to the effect that you didn't believe I discovered the space-craft?''

Foucault returned with seven glasses and the magnum of champagne on a silver tray. He passed the drinks around, smiling politely at Brecht. Then set the tray down on a cocktail table and took up the seventh glass.

Finally addressed himself to Brecht, ''Now really, it isn't very believable, you have to admit.''

Brecht shrugged and reached into an inner pocket of the suit he was now wearing. They had all changed from the space coveralls that were the uniform on Luna to more fashionable attire shortly before setting down at the spaceport. He brought forth a couple of the photos and handed them to their skeptical host. As expected, Foucault's eyes widened in disbelief.

''Good heavens, this tastes good,'' Mary Lou said, ''Just imagine, we don't have to worry about our liquor intake any more. We don't have to worry about coming down with space cafard. We don't have to worry about *anything*.''

''Ha!'' Brett-James said grimly. ''Yawl are dreaming, I shouldn't doubt. You don't think we're going to convince anybody down here that the Kraut didn't tell the rest of us where that damn spaceship is, do you? I say, wait until they've put the jolly old thumbscrews to you.''

Brecht finished off his glass of champagne and reached for the bottle. Foucault was still staring at the photos and shaking his head.

Zimmerman said, ''Better take it easy on this stuff. We're not used to a lot of booze and we don't know how long it will be before the bad guys show up. Or are they supposed to be the good guys?"

Brett-James looked at Foucault. "Which reminds me. . . . What is the drill, old chap? When are we scheduled to be put through the bloody wringer?"

"A doctor from the Ozma Department will arrive very shortly, as soon as you have, ah, caught your breaths. He will examine you—purely routine. If he feels you are sufficiently fit, you will have your preliminary interview with Director Vogel, the President of United America . . ."

"The President!" Mary Lou exclaimed.

". . . the Premier of Common Europe, the Foreign Minister of the Soviet Complex, and the Foreign Minister of the People's Republic of China."

"And no one else?" Brecht asked in a flat voice. "These five men, and yourself, are the only ones that have been let in on the—the secret?"

"That is correct," Foucault said. "The only reason I'm in on it is that somebody has to run interference for you. If anyone at all shows up who can't be avoided, such as the waiters or the maids who maintain the suite, I will always be present."

"I note that you're heeled too," Zimmerman commented mildly.

Foucault looked sharply at the Israeli, then nodded. "When I received my instructions from Director Vogel he told me that this is the most important development that has ever occurred in the history of the human race. I am to protect you with my life, especially Señor Brecht.''

''Very dramatic,'' Brecht muttered, pouring himself another glass of wine, despite Zimmerman's advice. He eyed the French-Moroccan. ''You mean to tell me that not even the Secretary General of the Reunited Nations is in on this?''

''That is correct,'' Foucault said again as he sipped his own wine appreciatively. ''The four nations named all have space programs; none of the others do.''

Azikiwe Awolowo, her dark face angry, snapped, ''Then the majority of the human race is not even to be told of this supposedly most important development that has ever happened to our species?''

''This is correct, Doctor Awolowo,'' he said for the third time. He shrugged. ''I did not make the rules. I'm a flunky whose two principal attributes are that I am connected with the Ozma Department and hence am up on the subject of space and its exploration and that I once won an Olympic gold medal for handguns.''

''When do we eat?'' Mary Lou put in. ''I'm starved, and although this wine is delicious, it's beginning to get to me.''

Foucault was immediately contrite. ''My sincere apologies,'' he said. ''I am an inadequate host.'' He hurried from the room.

''Is he our host or the butler? I can't keep track,'' said Zimmerman.

''Don't be a snob, Kike,'' Mary Lou said. ''Who cares if the butler sits down and helps you drink the champagne?''

When the French-Moroccan returned approximately fifteen minutes later, he was followed by four waiters pushing carts. They were accompanied by two of the guards who had remained out in the hall. As usual, their right hands were under their jackets.

Foucault said to the Luna team, "Please do not speak while these others are present and please remain seated where you are."

"I say, what bullshit," Brett-James muttered.

The French-Moroccan ignored him and led his group through the room and into what the six assumed was the suite's dining room. In no more than five minutes, the parade returned, the carts empty, the eyes of the waiters straight ahead, their expressions frozen. They marched out and were gone.

Their Man Friday, as he had named himself, returned and with his ever-present smile, gestured and announced, "Ladies and gentlemen, luncheon is served."

The food was exquisite, the first they had eaten under normal conditions for over five months.

Brecht said to Mary Lou, "You know, Yawl, this is considerably finer cuisine than you used to come up with on the moon. I'm beginning to have second thoughts about marrying you."

"No appreciation," Mary Lou muttered, digging in with the same gusto being exhibited by the others.

Zimmerman addressed Foucault, who was serving them, "What would have happened if, when those four characters came through pushing the carts, I had suddenly yelled, 'Guess what, there's an alien spaceship up on the damned moon!'? "

The other poured more claret for the Israeli, then said easily, "I am glad that you didn't, Doctor Zimmerman. I am not sure, but I assume that all four of them and the two guards who accompanied them would have been detained under top security conditions. I assume it would have been most uncomfortable for them in solitary confinement."

Zimmerman looked at Brecht sourly. "Listen, Kraut, why the hell didn't you just blow the damn thing up and forget about it?"

Brecht took a deep breath. "I'll tell you something, Kike, for a long time I considered doing just that."

Foucault looked from one to the other. "Kraut . . . Kike. : . ?"

Azikiwe laughed. "You see, we're all pretty close, and we have affectionate nicknames for each other," she explained.

CHAPTER SIX

FOLLOWING THE MEAL, they returned to the living room for a short time, then Foucault showed them about the suite and had them choose their bedrooms. He showed no particular surprise when Azikiwe selected a room with Brett-James, Li Ching with Zimmerman, and Brecht with Mary Lou. He went himself to get their luggage, which had evidently been delivered to the reception room.

The women especially ohhed and ahhed about the size of the suite, and about the view of the city from the living room window. None of them had ever been quartered so splendidly.

The feeling of apprehension still lay over them like a pall, however, and the increased gravity was with them as well, so they soon staggered back to the living room and allowed their guardian to bring them liqueurs by way of a digestive.

There was the tinkle of a bell and Foucault hurried to the door. He returned with a feisty-looking, middle-aged man, who carried two doctor's bags. The guards who accompanied him turned and left.

When the door was closed behind them, the newcomer said to Foucault indignantly, "Do you realize that when this examination is over I am to be detained indefinitely? That I am to be confined without any communication whatsoever, even with members of my family?"

"Yes," Foucault agreed pleasantly. "But I trust it will be only a short time, actually, and that you will be most fully recompensed. And here are your patients." He presented the six by name. "If I am not mistaken, you are Doctor Oswaldo Klein, of Vienna."

"Correct," the newcomer snapped. "Now, what is all this mumbo jumbo about?"

The French-Moroccan said gently, "Undoubtedly, Doctor, you have already been informed that your conversation is to be limited strictly to medical matters."

Klein snorted, "Very well. Which room can I utilize for the examinations? I'll take Ms. Pickett first."

Foucault shook his head smilingly. "It is necessary that the whole group, including me, remain together, Doctor."

The other stared at him. "As you know, this is a physical examination."

"As you know, this Luna City team has lived together in the greatest intimacy for five months. As for me, I'll turn my back, but I'll be present."

"Utter nonsense!" the doctor exclaimed.

The examinations proved to be cursory. They were all, on the face of it, in top physical shape.

He wound up by telling them gruffly, "You should have no difficulty. A mere two or three days should relieve you of any current gravity problems.'' He looked at Max Zimmerman approvingly. ''You must have had an excellent exercise program on Luna, Doctor.''

Li Ching said indignantly, ''He worked us to a frazzle.''

''You do not appear to be in a frazzle, my dear. You are a very attractive young woman.''

''Listen to the man, Chink,''

The doctor blinked at him. ''Chink?'' He shook his head and took up his bags.

Foucault ushered him to the door and turned him over to the two guards who had remained in the reception room.

The six members of the team resumed their chairs.

Zimmerman said, ''All this treatment is fine, but you know what I feel like?''

They all eyed him.

''Those conspirators who were charged with planning the assassination of Abraham Lincoln. When they were in prison, and then when they went on trial, they had sacks over their heads so that they couldn't talk. And when they were executed, it was the same. The doctor who treated Booth's broken leg was placed in solitary confinement until he died. He was never allowed to be in a position of talking to someone about what Booth might have said to him.''

Brett-James glanced suggestively at the bar. ''I say, old chap, what happens now?'' he asked Foucault.

. ''Sorry, Commander Brett-James, I do not know.''

"Then I suggest we investigate the Scotch situation, don't you know? We might as well live it up before they throw us out of these digs."

Brecht grunted in sour deprecation. "I have a suspicion we're going to be in these digs for a long, long time."

By the time Foucault had brought them their Scotch and sodas, the bell tinkled again and he hurried to the door to the reception room.

Brecht said, his voice still sour, "After this is all over and they've given me the Nobel Prize, I think I'll hire our boy to be my butler."

"Nobel Prize?" Azikiwe echoed. "Listen, Kraut, they're more apt to award you a bullet in the head."

At this point Foucault returned with a group of five men; and even the seemingly easygoing French-Moroccan was obviously impressed. The five were attired in very conservative business suits. The average age was sixty, and all five were men born to command.

They lined up in a row. The Luna team had already risen to their feet.

Foucault said formally, "Doctor Azikiwe Awolowo, Ms. Mary Lou Pickett, Doctor Li Ching, Commander Kingsley Brett-James, Doctor Max Zimmerman, Doctor Werner Brecht; may I present you to Their Excellencies, President Seymour Rice of United America, Premier Olaf Gunther of Common Europe, Foreign Minister Yul Konov of the Soviet Complex, Foreign Minister Yuan Lung of the People's Republic of China, and Director Nilsson Vogel of the Ozma Department of the Reunited Nations."

Yuan Lung nodded to Li Ching. "I knew your illustrious father, Comrade Li."

She bobbed her head. "He has mentioned your name with great respect many times in our home, Comrade Yuan."

President Seymour Rice's well-known qualities were immediately evident; his beaming face, his magnetic personality, his hearty masculinity, his notoriously mild intelligence were all apparent.

Since they were in United America, he assumed the role of host. "Shall we be seated, ladies and gentlemen?" He looked at Foucault. "You, my man, could you take orders for refreshments?"

"Yes, Mr. President, of course."

All now seated, with cocktails near at hand—orange juice in the case of the representative of the People's Republic—Olaf Gunther, of Common Europe, was the first to speak; in Esperanto, of course.

"If I understand correctly, Doctor Brecht, you are the geologist who inadvertently made the alleged discovery."

"Yes, Your Excellency."

"Frankly, I do not believe it." He was a heavy man, his face granite hard.

Werner Brecht reached into his pocket and brought forth the photos. He put them on the large cocktail table around which they all sat and leaned back, his dark eyes bright. The snapshots were sufficient in number that each of the world leaders could immediately peruse two or three before handing them around to the others.

Yul Konov said, "It looks like a Vostok."

"Superficially," Brecht replied. "But look at the photo that Premier Gunther has. That's me —in a spacesuit, of course—up against it. The Vostok wasn't nearly that size. Also notice those nubby antennae, or whatever they are; the Vostok didn't have any such thing. Besides, it's not metal, so far as I know, and it's not what you might call plastic, nor is it ceramic. I don't know what it is and I rather doubt that anybody on Earth would either."

Yul Konov leaned forward. "Doctor Brecht, this has come as a shock to all of us, I am sure. You have, thus far, revealed few details. According to Director Vogel, you have actually refused to disclose the location of the spacecraft."

"Yes, Your Excellency."

There was a moment's silence.

Then President Rice snapped, "Why, for God's sake?"

He told them substantially the same story he had told his five companions in Luna City on the occasion of his revelation of the existence of the spaceship from beyond the solar system.

When they had heard him out, Olaf Gunther said testily, "Doctor Brecht, has it not occurred to you that it might be better to leave the decision to more competent, wiser persons?"

"Yes, it has," Brecht agreed. "But what more competent, wiser persons? Yourselves? You represent the world's most powerful nations, and not one of you trusts any one of the others. You're all armed to the teeth with nuclear weapons, all ready to spring. I don't know what technology is in the space vehicle, but I don't trust it in the hands of the governments of any of your nations."

Director Vogel said, his heavy Swedish accent coming through the Esperanto, "Doctor Brecht, you are an employee of the Ozma Department. I order you to reveal the location of——"

"I just resigned," Brecht growled.

"You are under contract."

"I just broke it."

"That would void your pension."

Brecht stared at him in disgust. "I have the possible fate of the human race in my hands and you threaten me with something as meaningless and trivial as voiding my pension. Do you think I give a damn about my pension?"

The Director shifted unhappily in his chair and for the time said no more.

The Soviet Minister spoke up. "Let us not be too abrupt. I, for one, am flabbergasted. Has anyone come up with any theories about just why this sputnik from space landed itself on our moon?

"I understand it is thought to be millions of years old." He looked at Director Vogel.

"Yes, if Brecht's story is true. The rock he took from under it was turned over to a representative of my department and was fully tested in our laboratories. It is assumed to be at least as old as the period when life first appeared on Earth. I might mention at this point that this will give a considerable boost to directed panspermia theory research."

Yuan Lung said politely, "I am afraid that I am

not acquainted with the theory you mention."

Vogel turned to him. "The term was first used by a Swedish chemist, Svante Arrhenius. As far back as 1908, he suggested that living cells floated haphazardly through the universe, bringing life to suitable planets."

"Ridiculous," President Rice snorted. "Why, they'd freeze to death out there in space."

The Director faced him. "In the 1970s . . . the theory was expanded by Francis Crick, who earlier had won the Nobel Prize for helping discover the structure of DNA, the master molecule of life. With Leslie Orgel, of Stalk Institute, he advanced the possibility that life had come to this planet by spaceship, a deliberate act of seeding.

"They started with the question of why there is only one genetic code for terrestrial life. If life sprang up in some great 'primeval soup' as most biologists assume, it is surprising that a number of organisms with different codes do not exist. Crick and Orgel said that the existence of a single code seemed to be entirely compatible with the theory that all life descended from a single instance of directed panspermia."

He paused for a moment before going on. "They also noted that molybdenum plays a major role in many enzymatic reactions that are significant to life. Yet this element is rare, much less abundant than, say, nickel or chromium which are relatively umimportant in biochemical reactions. Because the chemical composition of organisms reflects to some extent the composition of the environment in which they evolved, thus

Crick and Orgel suggested that Earth life could have begun on a planet where molybdenum is more abundant.''

"It's not as farfetched as it might seem at first," Max Zimmerman mused. "Even today, our technology has reached the point where we could do some panspermia experiments of our own. Microorganisms, such as dormant algae and bacterial spores suitably protected and maintained at temperatures close to absolute zero, could be kept alive for hundreds of thousands of years. We could send them out in space probes that might someday orbit the planets of other star systems."

The Soviet Foreign Minister asked, "But why bother?"

Zimmerman shrugged. "I wouldn't know. Possibly Crick and Orgel were right: I read an article of theirs while still in medical school in which they postulated it was just some form of missionary zeal, this spreading of life throughout the galaxy."

"I came to some sort of similar conclusion myself," Brecht put in. "We have here a spaceship which comes from we know not where. Let's say it orbited Earth and dropped its load of life forms into the oceans. Its task supposedly completed, why didn't it simply drop down to Earth itself? The reason is that its task wasn't—and isn't—completed. It dared not drop down to Earth for fear that the life it seeded might destroy it."

He looked at each of them.

The spacecraft took off for the moon, and deliberately hid itself in that cave. How it possibly could have done so is one of the things that astonishes me. It must be fantastically sophisticated. But why? That we can answer. Why . . . because it knew it had a long wait and wanted to be safe from meteorites. What was it waiting for? It was waiting for the life it seeded to evolve to the point where it had a technology advanced enough to travel to the moon, to discover the spaceship and to open it."

"What's inside?" the Premier of Common Europe demanded.

Brecht hesitated. Then he said carefully, "I suspect that inside is information beyond our wildest dreams: their technology and science, presented in such a manner that we can decipher and utilize it."

President Rice was indignant. "Confound it then, man, don't you see that we must take immediate steps to open the damned thing? You owe it to the human race, to Earth, to reveal its location." His voice had risen to an inspired level, the way it did when he was soliciting votes.

Brecht shook his head impatiently. "You see, the intelligent beings who sent that fantastically advanced vessel through space to us made one mistake. It was a very basic mistake: they assumed that before a technological culture would reach the point where it could send its own space probes to its moon, it would have achieved civilization."

Once again, everyone was staring at him, his own teammates as well as the distinguished visitors.

"But we haven't," he finished simply.

CHAPTER SEVEN

KINGSLEY BRETT-JAMES laughed. "Bloody well told."

The Premier of Common Europe, of which the Englishman was a citizen, glared at him murderously, which affected that worthy not at all.

"The party is getting dry. How about a refill?" Zimmerman said to Foucault.

While the four leaders and Director Vogel eyed Brecht in frustration, Foucault went for another round.

Brecht said, "I want to know what the world is going to do with that spacecraft up there before I reveal where it is. And the answer had better be good. So far, we're off to a bad start: you haven't informed the press that it's there; you haven't even let the General Secretary of the Reunited Nations in on it, though I'll admit it's a pretty sterile organization."

Foreign Minister Yuan Lung, who up until now had largely kept his peace, said softly, "We have some very effective truth serum in the People's Republic."

Li Ching winced.

"So have we," said Yul Konov. He smiled meaningfully.

"We'll use our own truth serum," President Rice said. He added politely, "We should get about this immediately and it would take too long to import yours. I am sure they are all equally effective."

Brecht was on his feet. "I am not a national of any of your countries. I am a citizen of Peru and demand the opportunity to get in communication with my embassy."

Olaf Gunther looked at him musingly. "It occurs to me, from your name, that your background is European. There might be legal aspects putting you under our jurisdiction."

Brecht flushed angrily. "My German grandfather migrated to Peru and married a half-Spanish, half-Indian woman. My father married a full-blooded Peruvian Indian. I am not even half European—as though that makes any goddamned difference."

President Rice said smoothly, "Gentlemen, gentlemen, it is not a problem. The good doctor is in the United American Republic and consequently under our jurisdiction and subject to arrest."

"I'm beginning to feel sick," Mary Lou said, looking at her lover in despair.

"What's the charge?" Zimmerman asked.

Brecht was heartened to hear his team uniting behind him.

"I am sure our F.B.I. can come up with some suitable charge."

Azikiwe Awolowo spoke up for the first time.

"How about breaking and entering?" she said angrily.

Gentle, soft-spoken Li Ching snapped contemptuously, "How about rape?"

Brett-James said softly, "According to the Thoughts of Mao, rape is impossible. A girl with her dress up can run faster than a man with his pants down."

Gunther glared at him again. "This is hardly a time for levity."

"To the contrary," Zimmerman said coldly, "this thing is becoming more laughable by the minute and I, personally, am rapidly coming to agree with the stand that my colleague has taken."

"So am I," Azikiwe said. "When he first told us, there in the Luna Hilton, about the existence of the extraterrestrial ship, I thought Doctor Brecht was quite mad not to immediately announce it. But after this conversation, I am having second thoughts. I too would like to know what the world plans to do with it before it is turned over to what could lead to a four-way conflict for its possession."

"Ditto, by George," Brett-James murmured.

Foreign Minister Yuan got to his feet. Looking down at the photos, he said politely, "For some reason, I still cannot quite believe the story." He looked up at President Rice. "However, the truthfulness of the statement and the location of the spaceship will undoubtedly come out in the examination under truth serum. I assume you intend to make the investigation immediately?"

The President beamed. "In anticipation, I have

already taken measures. The Octagon has sent over the dosage.''

''Very well. I assume my Embassy will be immediately informed of the results. Meanwhile, I shall report to my superiors.'' He turned to Li Ching. ''You will report to the Embassy of the People's Republic at your earliest convenience, Comrade Li.''

''No!'' rapped Vogel.

''Doctor Li is a citizen of the People's Republic, Director.''

President Rice said unhappily, ''But until we have examined Brecht it is not actually known whether or not he has revealed the location of the spaceship to any of this companions.''

The Foreign Minister bobbed his head in a quick bow. ''I am willing to wait until the examination has taken place. If it is revealed that Doctor Li does not know the location, I request her presence at the Embassy.''

''And I'd like to talk to Commander Brett-James at the Common Europe Embassy,'' Olaf Gunther snapped.

''Gentlemen, let us compromise,'' Vogel said. ''Tomorrow morning, if it is found that they are unacquainted with the location, Doctor Li and Commander Brett-James will be escorted, under guard, to your respective embassies. You will take over their security while they are inside. After two hours they will be released and returned under guard to the Reunited Nations Building until this whole matter is solved. Agreed?''

They finally nodded.

The visitors stood, preparatory to leaving. Director Vogel remained seated, still eyeing Brecht malevolently.

The President said, "I will send up the serum immediately." To the other three leaders, "I suggest that we withdraw and have a conference among ourselves."

None of them bothered to make their farewells to the Luna team.

When they were gone, Zimmerman looked around at the others and said, "What happens now?"

Nobody seemed to know.

"Another drink?" Foucault suggested brightly.

Zimmerman asked, "What did you say your full name was?"

"Jean Hippolyte Foucault."

"I thought Hippolyte was the Queen of the Amazons. Isn't that a girl's name?"

Foucault smiled. "I'm half girl—on my mother's side."

Azikiwe laughed. She looked at their Man Friday appreciatively. "You're beginning to shape up."

Director Vogel opened his mouth but then closed it again.

"Let's have that drink," Mary Lou said, resignation in her voice. "We might as well get smashed."

By the time Foucault had served them all, save Vogel, who had shaken his head in disgust, the bell tinkled again and the French-Moroccan hurried to the door.

He returned with Doctor Oswaldo Klein, who had but one bag with him this time. They watched him withdraw a hypodermic.

He said, irritated again, "I'll be damned if I know what's going on but my instructions are to give Werner Brecht this shot."

In resignation, Brecht rolled up his sleeve.

Zimmerman snapped, "As Doctor Brecht's physician I refuse to allow him to take that shot. He has not been back on Earth more than a few hours and——"

"It's all right, Kike," Brecht said wearily. "They'd just bring in some of those bully-boys and I'd get it anyway with a few bruises to boot."

After he'd taken the injection and rolled down his sleeve again, he asked, "How long does it take to work?"

"Practically immediately," the doctor said, snapping his medical kit shut. He looked around. "I'd like to know what the hell's going on around here."

"That will be all, Doctor Klein," Vogel said ominously.

The doctor turned and was escorted out by Foucault.

Director Nilsson Vogel waited a full ten minutes before he took up the questioning. The others remained silent, sipping their drinks. What was there to say?

Vogel began finally, addressing himself directly to Brecht, "You claim that you found and photographed an extraterrestrial spaceship on the surface of Luna?"

"Yes."

"Is that true?"

"Yes."

"Where was it?"

"It was under a rock ledge in what amounted to almost a cave."

"Where is the rock ledge located?"

"I can't tell you."

They all gawked at him.

Vogel snapped, "Why not?"

Brecht said reasonably, "There aren't exactly any road maps on Luna, you know. I could take you there, but I couldn't explain to you where it is."

"There are aerial photos of the moon, taken when the Ozma program was first planned."

Brecht sighed. "Do you know the difference between an aerial photo and jockeying a Luna vehicle around those rocks and crags, those stark hills and gullies and sand dunes? I could no more point it out on an aerial photo than I could levitate."

"How far is it from Luna City?"

The Peruvian thought about that. "I'd say as the crow flies, perhaps five or six miles. As the sand buggy crawls, possibly as much as ten."

The other was silent for several minutes. Finally he said, "Did you take any of your companions to it or tell them where it is located?"

"No."

"Is there anything, anything at all, that you can tell me that would indicate the location of this spaceship?"

"No, there isn't."

Brett-James laughed at the Director's obvious frustration.

"Shut up!" Vogel snapped, then got to his feet

and stomped out of the room. He was obviously in a rage.

Mary Lou said, "How about another drink?"

Brecht looked at her. "Now there's a facet of your personality I didn't know about. I'd been thinking of making an honest woman of you, after I've won my Nobel Prize. But a female alcoholic. . ."

"I still say they'll shoot you, Kraut. No Nobel Prize," Azikiwe said.

Mary Lou was looking at Brecht thoughtfully. "Make an honest woman out of me, eh? Listen, while that truth serum is still working, answer this: do you love me?"

"Yes."

"I'll be damned," said Mary Lou.

Zimmerman said, "Let's take a pool. I'll bet ten pseudo-dollars that the whole story's on TV news by morning."

They eyed him, frowning.

He shrugged. "This is all a damn farce, this secret bit. We six, Foucault the Amazon here, the Director and four world leaders are supposedly the only ones in on it. Ha! The President will take it up with his aides; he obviously hasn't the brains to think out anything himself. How many aides will he talk to? The two foreign ministers will have to relay it on to their governments. How many will be brought in to debate the alleged secret? Gunther is Premier of Common Europe. How many member governments will he have to bring it up to? Twenty? How many countries are there in Common Europe? Damned if I know."

"So?" Brett-James said.

"So I say it will leak before morning. And then, as somebody observed, the manure will hit the fan."

CHAPTER EIGHT

IT WAS SHEER luck that none of them had taken Max Zimmerman's bet; they would have lost.

As they straggled into the living room the next morning, they found Brett-James in front of the TV screen, laughing his head off at a face dark with righteous anger, above a reversed collar, sounding off in tones of rage.

Zimmerman and Li Ching entered together. "What's up, Your Majesty?"

Brett-James dialed the set down and turned to them, still chuckling. "I've got some kind of Fundamentalist bishop on. He's hit the ceiling, don't you know? Says that it's all a hoax. Life was created, so and so many thousand years ago—he has it down to the day—by God, along with all the stars in the universe and Adam and Eve in the Garden of Eden. All this stuff about a spaceship that's been on the moon since before life started up in the oceans, is blasphemy."

Foucault came in, looking weary and harried, looking as though he'd been up all night. He said, "Somebody must have leaked it deliberately within an hour of leaving this suite. Damned if I know who, or why. But somebody among our top-secret boys evidently thought it would be better to spread the word. It's going around like a top. We're going to release the photos. No reason why not."

Werner Brecht entered. "What's up?"

Foucault answered, "The news is out. If any of you people want visitors, you're perfectly free to have them. The guards will be maintained and even reinforced but you are no longer what practically amounted to being prisioners. Frankly, I wouldn't suggest that any of you leave. Especially you, Doctor Brecht. There are some crackpot elements already calling for your neck."

"The damn fools!" Zimmerman exclaimed. "If anything happens to the Boche, they'll never find the damn thing."

Li Ching asked, "What's the serious side of the news?" Obviously every religion in the world is in a crisis. Practically all of them base their teachings on the fact that a god, or gods, created all life."

"Well, part of the news is that the newsmen are out in the reception room and crowded halfway down the halls. There seem to be hundreds of them." Foucault looked at Brecht. "You'd better start thinking your story through. I told them we'd let them in after breakfast. By the way, three or four of the magazines and news chains want to get in to see you first. They're offering big money for an exclusive."

"To hell with that," Brecht growled. "The moment I begin to make money out of this, the whole position I've assumed erodes." He looked at Brett-James. "What else is on the news, Your Majesty?"

70

"Well, the Chinese are in favor of using a bit of torture on you, old chap. They call it, ever so gently, putting you to the question. The Soviets seem to think it's a good idea. The American Civil Liberties Union is already up in arms in your defense. So is the Peruvian Embassy which, by the way, has demanded that you be released to their custody. The World Government League recommends that the whole world unite to meet the common problems."

"I'll stay where I am," Brecht said bitterly. "You don't know the kind of politicians we have in my country. They'd probably sell me to the Chinese. What's the World Government League?"

"Just what it sounds like," Zimmerman said. "They make some sense. There's not a hell of a lot of them but they're organized in just about every country."

In view of what had been said about torture, Li Ching was quick to add, "They are even in China, though underground. They are organized particularly among the intellectuals and professionals."

Mary Lou and Azikiwe were now present.

"The various UFO organizations are having a field day, don't you know?" Brett-James went on. "They're vindicated, by George! They say that not only was the Earth visited millions of years ago but it is continually being scouted by alien life forms. And, they ask most ominously, for what sinister purposes?"

"Jesus," Zimmerman said. "Let's have breakfast. There'll be hell to pay soon enough when we let those media boys in."

"Just one other item," Brett-James hastened to

71

add. "The Racial Purists demand to know whether or not you peeked inside, and, if so, was there any indication of the color or other racial characteristics of the occupants."

Brecht shook his head in amazement. "I don't know if there ever were any occupants. For all I know, the thing was robot controlled." He led the way to the dining room, as the bell tinkled.

Foucault went to answer it.

He returned with two strangers. He said to Brett-James, "They're here for you, Commander. From the Common Europe Embassy."

"Yes, of course," Brett-James affirmed, eyeing the breakfast paraphernalia regretfully.

The French-Moroccan turned back to the newcomers. "Your identification, please." They handed it over and he went to the phone screen and dialed the Embassy of Common Europe. "Please give me your security officer." He waited for a moment. "I have two men here at the Reunited Nations Building who have come for Commander Kingsley Brett-James. Will you please describe them for me in detail?" He listened and finally nodded. "Very well, thank you very much."

Kingsley Brett-James nodded too. "Perhaps I can get breakfast over there."

They were hardly out of the room when the phone screen hummed. Foucault raced for it. "Supposedly our calls are being screened. Nothing but really top priority."

He listened for a moment, then turned to Li Ching, frowning. "It's the Embassy of the People's Republic of China. They want you to report immediately, Doctor Li. I'll get guards for you."

"Certainly," she agreed, her voice low.

They left the room; only Foucault returned. "Well, how about breakfast? You'll probably all need it—especially you, Doctor Brecht. It's going to be quite a day. They're setting you up for television, among other things."

"Oh, great," Brecht muttered.

But the phone hummed again. Foucault answered it impatiently. His face registered concern as he turned to Mary Lou. "It's a message for you, Ms. Pickett, relayed from Hopewell, South Carolina. Your mother is very ill and calling for you."

Mary Lou darted for her bedroom, to return in moments with her bag.

Foucault was back on the phone. "Two guards immediately to escort Ms. Pickett to Hopewell, South Carolina. Use one of the Reunited Nations aircraft."

Azikiwe called, "Sorry, Mary Lou," but the American was gone.

The man behind the desk was not young. He said wearily "Commander Brett-James?"

"Yes, sir."

"Please be seated. It is a pleasure to meet you. I have seen snapshots of you as a baby, more times than I appreciated at that point."

"Sir?"

"I was your father's wing man, during what history now calls the Battle of Britain." His shoulders seemed to sag. "Looking back, we were little more than children ourselves. But we were in fighter craft, pursuit planes. Hurricanes.''

"Yes, sir,'' Brett-James said. "I knew that my father died in a Hurricane.''

"Yes, he did. It was my fault.''

Brett-James said nothing.

"It is a story too long to tell at this time. The Buzz-Bombs were coming in, the V-1s. They were very fast. You had time for one pass at one plane, then they were gone. There were six Heinkels in the vicinity but your father went in. You see, the Buzz-Bomb was headed for Petersberg, where his family—including you—and mine lived. He depended on me to cover him, since I was his wing man. He finished off the robot-craft and then when he saw I was having trouble with the Jerries, he came back. He shouldn't have. He had lost too much altitude. He was a sitting duck. He should have hit for home, hedge-hopping.''

The man sighed. "He was my best friend, Kingsley.'' He paused. "I am, by the way, Field Marshal Worthington. Retired, of course. Last night, in view of my former connections with your family, I was hurried from my home in Kent, put upon a supersonic plane, and sent here to plead with you.''

"Plead, sir?''

"You are an Englishman. Great Britian is now part of Common Europe, but you are still an Englishman. The nation that gets to that spacecraft first will dominate the world. I, for one, have no desire to be dominated by any of the other world powers. Commander Brett-James, we need your help.''

"Sir, I don't know where the extraterrestrial

spaceship *is*." He hesitated before adding, "Even if I did, I am not sure I would reveal it. I am rapidly coming to the same stand Doctor Brecht has taken."

The Field Marshal said urgently, "Commander, you now do not know where the spaceship is. But you are a close intimate of Brecht—every effort must be brought to bear——"

Kingsley Brett-James was on his feet, shaking his head.

After a second's pause, the older man also stood. He turned and faced the door behind him, but Brett-James could understand every word. "Commander, there is someone else who has flown from England to plead for your assistance. He is, of course, traveling incognito. May I present you to your sovereign, King Charles."

A middle-aged man attired in a business suit entered.

Commander Kingsley Brett-James snapped to attention.

Li Ching's two Reunited Nations guards parked themselves at the entrance to the Embassy of the People's Republic of China, and she went in alone.

She was obviously expected. Her escort was a nervous embassy official who conveyed her to an office occupied only by Foreign Minister Yuan Lung, who politely stood upon her entry. He dismissed her guide, then bowed slightly to his visitor.

"Welcome, Comrade Li," he said in Mardarin, not Esperanto.

She nodded. "Comrade Foreign Minister."

"Please be seated before the phone screen. There is a message from Peking for you."

Frowning, she sat in front of the screen. It lit up, and the face was well known to her, although she had never met the man.

"Comrade Li, the People's Republic is in danger. Our space program is not as advanced as that of the imperialist powers nor of the Soviet Complex. However, we have sufficient equipment to send a space vessel to Luna, excavate the visitor from the stars, and return it here to China. All Party members in a position to aid in this task must be utilized. If we are not the first to recover this spaceship, the People's Republic is doomed, Comrade Li. Foreign Minister Yuan Lung will give you the details of your task."

Li Ching said emptily, "Yes, Comrade Chairman."

The face faded.

Yaun Lung had been standing during the time the Chairman of the Communist Party of the People's Republic was talking. Now he reseated himself and regarded Li Ching thoughtfully. He said, "It is understood, Comrade Li, that before embarking to Luna, you were put under hypnosis to assure your complete affection for and cooperation with your colleagues from other countries."

"Yes, Comrade Yuan. All of us were. It is standard procedure in the Ozma Department."

"And you became the mistress of Doctor Zimmerman, who is presumably not sympathetic to the Party?"

"Yes, Comrade."

"It will be necessary, perhaps, to switch your

affiliation to Warner Brecht.''

''But——''

He said smoothly, ''We have our own doctors here, Comrade Li. They will return you to a hypnotized state and remove the post-hypnotic suggestions implanted in your mind. You will then be free to exercise your party duties without this insidious pressure. You will receive instructions from two of our security comrades. Among other things, they will give you some small pills. When you are alone with Werner Brecht, you will see that he takes one. Perhaps in a drink, preferably alcoholic; within five minutes it will act. It is a truth serum, devised by our comrade scientists. He will answer anything you ask him.''

Li Ching said miserably, ''But Comrade Yung, he does not know how to describe the location of the rock ledge where the vessel is hidden. He could lead someone there, but he couldn't describe the route.''

''Yes he could,'' the other insisted. ''This serum works on the subconscious as well as the conscious. At least it will elicit enough details to get us near enough to find the spaceship. For instance, does it lie to the north of the Observatory, or the south, east or west? Implanted in his mind is the exact route he takes to get to it. Have him describe, word for word, every turn he takes, every hill, every gully he crosses. You will be given a small electronic bug. His complete description of his path to the rock ledge will be recorded. It will be enough.''

He touched a button on his desk.

''That will be all, Comrade Li. The People's

Republic is depending upon you. Our security comrades will answer any questions you may have."

"But this isn't the way to the airport!"

"No, Ms. Pickett," the guard on her left replied. "We're going to the Octagon. So far as we know, there is nothing wrong with your mother's health."

"What?"

The other guard now spoke. "We wished to remove you from the Reunited Nations Building without your companions suspecting your real destination. It must be obvious to all of you that Commander Brett-James and Doctor Li Ching were taken to their embassies to be pressured into revealing whatever they can about the location of the spaceship. We don't want your companions, particularly Brecht, to know that your government is also soliciting help."

She said indignantly, "What a cruel manner in which to accomplish your mission. How do you think I felt when I got that message?"

Both of them nodded wearily. "This world is getting crueler by the minute, Ms. Pickett," one said. "How would you like the Soviet Complex or the People's Republic to have first grabs on the technological information that might be in that thing?"

She didn't answer.

They were waved through at the Octagon. The chauffeur of their limousine had opaqued the windows so that no one could see in. They sped down the guarded highway, into the guarded entry point, through the narrower, tunnel-like road in the interior, down the ramp to the autopark. A quartet of men, submachine gun armed, guarded the vicinity where the limousine came to a halt. Mary Lou emerged, followed by her two guards.

"This way, Ms. Pickett." One preceded her, his partner came behind, and the four armed men brought up the rear, looking this way and that way, as though momentarily expecting danger right there in the Octagon. It was the same silly ultra-security of the day before, she thought bitterly.

They wound their way through the basements eventually ending up at the door to a small office, through which she was ushered—alone. The occupant was standing when she entered.

She recognized him. In actuality, he was her ultimate boss.

He strode forward and shook her hand warmly. "Ms. Pickett, I am General Hugh Hoffman, of the American Space Program."

"Yes, I know."

"Please excuse the cavalier method by which you were brought here, Ms. Pickett." He spoke in English; his accent was the same as hers. He gestured her to a chair across from his desk, and returned to his own.

He regarded her for a moment, then said, "An ancestor of mine, a Colonel Hoffman, fell under your great-grandfather at the famous charge at Gettysburg, during the War Between the States."

She didn't know how to respond to that.

He mused, "My family has observed the military traditions ever since. My grandfather fought in the First World War, my father died with Patton in the Second. I myself fought as a young man in the Asian War. It is a noble tradition."

"I never thought much of the military myself," Mary Lou said tartly. "It turns people into professional killers. Something like robbers, only robbers don't particularly want to kill you; they just want your valuables. The military exists to kill people."

He leaned back and looked at her. "That's one way of seeing it," he acknowledged. "But how would you like the Russkies or the Gooks to get to that spaceship first, Ms. Pickett?"

She said, "I haven't the vaguest idea of what they might find inside."

"We don't either, but some of our double-domes have already come up with certain ideas. For instance, it would seem possible that a culture advanced enough to send a space probe to Earth might have a method of preventing nuclear explosions. With such information in our hands, a potential enemy would be at our mercy."

"What potential enemy?"

He sighed. "Ms. Pickett, the world has been at peace for some time, but it is a shaky peace. Our war with the Soviet Complex or possibly China will yet be fought. We need every advantage we can collect."

"What do you expect of me?"

"You sleep with Doctor Brecht, do you not?"

"Werner Brecht is my lover."

"Excellent," he told her. "You will remain tonight in an apartment here in the Octagon, to continue the pretense that you have flown to South

Carolina to see your mother. Tomorrow you will return to the Reunited Nations Building with the news that she has recovered. Doctor Brecht, we understand, is not particularly nationalistically inclined. As a patriotic American, you will do everything you can to persuade him to lead an *American* expeditionary force to the alien spacecraft."

CHAPTER NINE

LACKING ONLY MARY LOU, the team with Foucault in attendance were gathered around the large TV screen in the living room of the penthouse suite.

Werner Brecht was shaking his head in disbelief.

Senator Bull Armanroder was speaking. "If there is one intelligent species out there, there are most likely more. According to Shklovski and Sagan in their book *Intelligent Life in the Universe*, the number of civilizations substantially ahead of our own in this galaxy is perhaps between fifty thousand and one million. The Rand Corporation, in a detailed analysis done by Stephen Dole, determined the mathematical probability of fourteen stars within twenty-two light years of our sun that could have intelligent life. The nearest is Alpha Centauri A and B which are but four-point-three light years from Earth.

The Senator hesitated for a moment for emphasis. And then, "Friends, we must prepare to meet the challenge of these alien cultures. It has been postulated that aliens more advanced than we are would be less warlike, but that might be unrealistic. Fearing for their own security, they might blast us with super-weapons from these space probes which we already know they have. They might use biological fumigation, or they might even have the power to trigger an explosion in our sun, turning it into a nova which would bake the Earth.

"Friends, United America must prepare. We must begin construction of a space fleet to patrol outer space and turn aside any potential enemies. We must find new weapons, greater weapons than the H-Bomb.

"If and when we make contact with the aliens, we must work out some kind of weapons systems limitations with them. We might possibly work toward an agreed number of spacecraft permissible in certain volumes of space . . ."

"Jesus Christ," Max Zimmerman exclaimed in disgust.

". . . We could keep the communications channel open, an interstellar hot line to prevent a misunderstanding of events, such as an off-course spaceship."

Brecht reached out and dialed another station. "An interstellar hot line, yet. What a hot line! It would take four-point-three years minimum to get a message one way, another four-point-three years to get an answer. "What a mentality!"

Zimmerman said slowly, "There are some other angles on that, Kraut. A lot of capable scientists have been speculating on this whole thing. A Professor Gerald Feinberg did a paper called 'On the Possibility of Faster Than Light Particles' in which he points out that the theory of relativity doesn't say that nothing can travel faster than light; it says nothing can travel *at* the speed of light. Feinberg points out that the speed of light is a limiting velocity, but a limit has two sides. He imagines entities which can *only* travel faster than light. The problem would be, of course, to jump over the speed of light barrier to the other side.''

"Hold it, hold it," Brett-James protested. "I'm getting a headache, old chap.''

Zimmerman continued heedlessly, "There are electronic devices now which accomplish roughly the same thing. The Tunnel diode is an example: electrons tunnel from one side of an electrical barrier to the other without going through it.''

"What's all this in aid of?" Brecht asked.

Zimmerman shrugged. "Possibly those aliens are not limited in either communication or transport to the speed of light. Possibly that spaceship you found has been there only a few years, or even less, and right this minute is beaming information about Earth back to its home planet.''

"But that rock Brecht found was millions of years old," Li Ching protested.

Zimmerman nodded. "But the spaceship was on top of the rock; the rock wasn't on top of the spaceship. There are tons of rocks on the surface of the moon that are millions of years old. The ship could have landed at any time. It doesn't prove anything about how long it's been there simply by sitting on something millions of years old.''

"To get back to that silly senator . . ." Azikiwe said sourly, ". . .it's not just the Americans. They're all beating the war drums—as though interstellar cultures should be dealt with in the same manner as our primitive Earthside international politics. When are we going to grow up?"

Brecht said, "I'd think it's rather a basic assumption that as a culture achieves ultra-technology, with it would go tolerance and compassion. I should think that eventually, when we contact our superiors out there among the stars, we need have nothing to fear save our own shortcomings. At this point we are a rather simple culture."

Brett-James said lightly, "According to the Thoughts of Mao, the simple things of life are the most satisfying. Sleeping soundly, breathing clean invigorating air, drinking clean fresh water . . . girls."

Li Ching flushed. "Chairman Mao never said anything like that," She spat out angrily.

Brett-James' eyes widened in surprise. "I apologize and all that. It must have been George Washington who said it, or possibly Buddah."

Azikiwe said hastily, "I think I'm going to join that World Government League."

"What's *their* stand?"

"Form a valid world government; persuade the Kraut, here, to reveal the spaceship's location; investigate its contents to see if we can learn anything—technologically; open up contact with the aliens as soon as possible. In general, play it by ear."

"Makes more sense than anything else I've heard so far." Brecht stood up. "The hell with it. I'm going to bed. Good night, all."

Zimmerman was saying, "What do you think, Chink?"

Li Ching said flatly, "The word Chinese is derived from Ch'in, a dynasty that preceded the Christian era. I am a Han, not a Ch'in, not to speak of being a Chink."

Max Zimmerman was clearly taken aback. "Jesus! Sorry."

Brecht went on to his room. Silently, his face expressionless, he undressed. Since Mary Lou was gone to see her mother in South Carolina and there would be no bed companion for him tonight, he donned pajamas. But instead of getting under the covers and seeking sleep, he stretched out on top of them, put his hands behind his head, and stared up at the ceiling.

He didn't know if things were going the way he wanted them to or not. Originally, he had expected the discovery he had reported to be taken immediately to the Reunited Nations. Although the news media had it in full now, thus far the world organization had had nothing to say. Possibly it was because the major powers controlled it.

He was still musing some fifteen minutes later when a knock came at the door. He was puzzled but he called, "Come on in, the door's unlocked."

And Li Ching entered.

Dressed in a diaphanous wisp of a nightgown, she bore a tray with an open bottle of champagne and two glasses, both full. She put the tray down on the night table between the beds and went back to lock the door before returning to sit on the twin bed across from him. Her face was slightly flushed and her almond eyes downcast.

Brecht was astonished. "What in the world, Li Ching . . . ?"

Her voice was low, hesitant. "It occurred to me that you might be lonesome tonight, especially in view of all the pressure on you these days, and that perhaps you might like a nightcap, Werner."

He had always found her superlatively attractive, even though he had chosen Mary Lou Pickett to be his bed companion in the Luna Hilton.

He looked at her now, sitting there on the edge of his bed, her nightgown nearly transparent. "Werner, eh? Not the Kraut? Not the Boche?"

She tightened her lips infinitesimally and said, "I think those nicknames are somewhat ridiculous, Werner. You're not even a German. Here, darling, would you like a sip of wine? It's pleasantly cold."

"No—not yet, at least." He looked into her face a long time before speaking again and she began to flush a little. "How about Max, Li Ching? I thought you were in love with him."

She shrugged her slight shoulders. "That was a temporary arrangement, for our time on the moon. Surely none of us thought of it as permanent. When you had your other two tours of duty, didn't you have temporary women companions that you gave up once you returned to Earth?"

"Yes, of course," he replied. "Once a Dutch girl, and once a Yugoslavian."

"Well . . ." She cast her eyes down. "Don't you like me?"

"I always have, Li Ching. Come over here."

She hesitated for the briefest moment, before crossing to him. She glanced at the wine in despair as she sat beside him.

He ran one hand up the almost golden leg and

pulled her head down. She gasped slightly, then let him kiss her. Her passion grew with his fondling, her eyes on his.

Although he had been restraining himself thus far, partly because his mind had been so concentrated on other things earlier, partly because he felt like a bit of a heel, now the pleasure and demands of the sex act took over and he could think of nothing save the petite woman next to him.

When it was over, she stretched out by his side, breathing deeply.

"Do . . . do you love me?"

He said gently, "The same as I have always loved you, Li Ching."

"But—but now . . ."

He said nothing.

She hung her head for a moment, then took a deep breath. "That made me terribly thirsty. Would you like some of the wine now?"

He looked at her and shook his head. "Li Ching, you make a lousy seductress. I am afraid that it isn't in your character."

"I . . . I don't know what you mean." She came to her feet and stared down at him. There was desperation in her eyes. Desperation, hurt, and shame. She gave it one last try. Picking up one of the glasses of champagne, she said, "Here, darling."

Brecht sighed deeply. "What's in the champagne, Li Ching? Is the People's Republic of China trying to poison me? A slug of poison delivered to me by one of the people I like most in this world."

Her slight shoulders sagged. "Oh, no, Werner.

Not poison—not from me. It is a truth serum. It was hoped that under its influence you would reveal the location of the extraterrestrial craft. The government of my people desperately wish to find it before the imperialist powers do. They will use its contents only for honorable purposes."

"Of course," Brecht said. "So would any of the other rival powers if they were to get to it first."

"But . . . but you *must* understand, Werner! The People's Republic has no ulterior motives."

"So I see. Even though they tried to make a whore of you to gain their ends." He sighed. "Good night, Li Ching. I'm sorry it worked out this way. No hard feelings—you did what you thought was your duty. By the way . . ."

She was hanging her head.

"You look really cute in that outfit. And it was an awfully good experience. But, in spite of it all, I'm in love with Mary Lou. Good night again, Li Ching."

Right at the door, she turned and frowned at him. "How did you know?" she asked.

He gave a sour little laugh. "Li Ching, Li Ching . . . it was obvious you had been brainwashed at the Chinese Embassy, or rather, de-brainwashed, so that you would no longer feel affection toward the rest of us. Otherwise you wouldn't have spoken so sharply to Brett-James. Nor would you have objected to Max calling you a Chink. If they brainwashed you, it must have been to some purpose. What? There was only one purpose. And their need was to wipe away your subconscious affection for me."

"If so, they failed," Li Ching said softly. She unlocked the door and was gone.

He muttered, "Poor kid."

Max Zimmerman strolled in about ten minutes later. "Saw your light on, and thought I'd drop by," he said. "I can't stand any more of that TV crap." He stretched out on the other twin bed. "You know what I think the Americans are building up to?"

"No, what?"

"Twisting your arm, Kraut. Making you take them up to the extraterrestrial ship. They're one up on everybody else. They got you under their thumb: you're not in Moscow, or Peking, or wherever; you're right here in Greater Washington."

Brecht grunted. "If they tried it, Common Europe, the Soviet Complex, or China, or perhaps all three, would hit them," he said.

"Probably," Zimmerman admitted. Then, irrelevantly he asked, "What would you do if you had a hundred million pseudo-dollars, Kraut?"

"A hundred million? In my time I've wished I was a millionaire, but a hundred million . . ." Brecht laughed. "I couldn't put a dent in a hundred million if I lived to be two hundred."

"I'd help you spend it."

"Here, have a glass of champagne. It's still cold," Brecht offered.

The other took the glass and said, "Jesus, you Peruvians really live it up. Champagne in bed, yet." He took a swallow and said, "Here's to the ladies." Then, "Think of all the ladies there'd be if you had a hundred million pseudo-dollars."

"I've got all the lady I want."

"A very narrow way of looking at it." Zimmerman emptied his glass. "You're not drinking."

"No. Who got to you, Kike?"

The timber of the Israeli's voice changed infinitesimally. "The Soviets," he said.

"How?" Brecht demanded. "You haven't left the suite."

"Through Foucault. He works for the KGB. Kind of a double agent."

"I see. What was the plan?"

"If you accepted the offer, to smuggle you out of here, over to the Soviet Complex, to lead a Soviet expedition to the alien spaceship."

"They would have had their work cut out, sneaking me out of here," Brecht said in disgust. "Why in the hell did you do it, Max?"

"Are you kidding?" A slice of a hundred million pseudo-dollars? I'm neither an American nor a Soviet and don't support either of their countries. It's not going to make any difference to me which one of them gets there first. It'll probably lead to war either way, and we'll all die. Meanwhile, I could be spending whatever portion of the hundred million you divvied up with me."

"Possibly makes some sense, Max, but it's no go. "Sorry."

Zimmerman swung his legs over the side of the bed, stood up and stretched. "That's what I thought you'd say." He yawned. "How'd you get me to open up so easily?"

"There was truth serum in the champagne," Brecht told him. He had returned to staring up at the ceiling.

"Well, good night again," Zimmerman called, heading for the door. "See you in the morning. I've got a sneaking suspicion old Vogel will be back to question you some more."

"Probably," Brecht muttered. He added bitterly, "I wonder who's next."

Next was Kingsley Brett-James.

He knocked, but entered before Brecht could speak. "Hallo, old chap. Something just came to mind that I think might be a bit urgent, don't you know."

"Oh, what's that?" The Peruvian gestured to the other bed.

"That spacecraft," Brett-James stated earnestly. "You're the only one who knows where it is, Kraut. What happens if something happens to you? And the way things are developing, something could, don't you know."

"I realize that." Brecht sighed. "If something happens to me, though, they'll never find it."

"That's what I mean," the Englishman said. "Kraut, the human race needs that vehicle. I've gone along with you thus far, but sooner or later, whatever's in that spaceship ought to be revealed."

"So?"

"On the face of it, old boy, you ought to tell one of us where it is. Surely you could give enough of a description of the route you take to get to it that one of us could find it."

"And you nominate yourself?"

The Britisher nodded, unwontedly serious. "Since I thought of the idea. The fewer who knew that I knew, the better. If you told someone else instead, there would be three of us in on it."

Brecht sighed. "Li Ching offered me her fair young body and champagne. Zimmerman offered me, believe it or Ripley, a hundred million pseudo-dollars. You don't offer me anything except a phony story. Your Majesty, tell your Common Europe superiors that it was a good try, but no dice. I'm keeping the location to myself."

Brett-James looked at him in frustration. "You're making a mistake, Brecht, dear boy."

"Could be."

When the Englishman was gone, Brecht put his hands behind his head again and stared up at the ceiling, waiting.

He thought, "Three down, one to go. At least Mary Lou is in South Carolina, where they can't get at her."

The knock sounded at the door only moments later.

Azikiwe Awolowo came in at his response. She was looking back over her shoulder. "Wasn't that His Majesty?"

"Yes," said Brecht. "He came in with the idea that in view of the fact that some crackpot might get it into his head to knock me off, I should reveal to at least one other person the location of the spaceship."

"Oh," she said, considering it. "Maybe that's a good idea at that."

"Yeah, but who?"

She was dressed in black slippers, black slacks, and a black turtlenecked sweater, and looked like a whole pile of million pseudo-dollar bills.

"That's a good question," she said.

"Stretch out and tell me all," Brecht said wearily, gesturing at the other bed. "Who got to you, Azikiwe?"

"How do you mean?" She lay down, copying him with her hands behind her head, staring up at the ceiling.

"Who wants you to try and wriggle out of me the location of the space probe?"

She was mildly surprised. "How in the hell did you know, Kraut? That's what I came in to talk to you about."

"I just know," he sighed.

"What the hell's going on here?" she said. "I came to tell you that the Afro-Asia Bloc tried to twist my arm earlier today to get you to open up."

"The Afro-Asian Bloc? Fer crissakes, why? None of them has a space program. They couldn't get to the moon to recover the damn thing even if they knew where it was." Brecht was surprised.

"I don't know," she answered. "I guess they're all caught up in the hysteria, or something. I went over to my Embassy just to check in, to make arrangements to transfer some of my credits home and that sort of thing."

"And what happened?"

"You'll never believe it. They grabbed me by the scruff of my black ass and hauled me up before a bunch of double-domes. They unscrambled that affection deal the Ozma Department medicos hypnotically implanted in us before we took off for Luna City. I don't love you—or any of the rest of the team—anymore, at least not in the same way I used to."

"Oh?" Brecht said, looking over at her. "How do you love us now?"

She grinned. "You'd be surprised. In actuality, just about the same as before. I'll have to figure it out, but I still like the whole team fine. Even that bastard Brett-James."

"Well, what the hell happened then?" Brecht was curious enough to raise himself up on an elbow and stare at her.

She shrugged. "What do you think happened? Nothing. They wanted to know if I knew where the damned thing is and I told them no. They wanted to know if there was any way I could wriggle the information out of you. I told them that I doubted it but even if I could I wouldn't, unless you told me on your own for whatever reason."

Brecht continued to stare at her. "And then what happened?"

"Oh, they tried getting a bit tough. They said my country depended on me, and I asked them in what way. And they said if they had the secret of the location of the space probe they could use it to pry advantages out of the great powers."

"Oh, Brother," Brecht groaned. "What a fouled-up mess that could become."

"That's what I told them," Azikiwe said. "But they're so up-tight they couldn't see it. It looks to me like the whole world is rapidly getting scrambled brains over this."

"Yeah," Brecht said, and lowered himself to his back once more.

She swung her legs around and sat up, looking at him mischievously. "If it wasn't for Mary Lou,

I've half a mind to climb in there with you."
He grinned back at her. "No thanks."

CHAPTER TEN

BRECHT SLEPT LATE, having found it difficult getting to sleep at all.

When he entered the living room, the others, minus Mary Lou, were all there, finished with breakfast. He went on through to the dining room and poured himself coffee and buttered half a Danish sweet roll. He went back to the living room, eating the roll, sipping at the coffee, and looked about him.

They seemed quite unrepentant.

He said conversationally, "The Nigger tells me that at her Embassy they removed the hypnotic suggestion that resulted in our having such an undying affection for one another. Li Ching and His Majesty, too. Right?"

Li Ching nodded. "The psychiatrists at the Embassy of the People's Republic worked on me. It's surprising how little effect it seems to have had."

"Ditto," Brett-James said.

"How about you, Kike?"

"Not me," the Israeli said cheerfully. "I still love you all to distraction, especially the girls."

"But not a hundred million pseudo-dollars

worth, eh?'' Brecht said sourly, washing down his Danish with the last last of the coffee.

Zimmerman pantomimed hurt feelings. ''I was going to split it with you. We would then have lived happily ever afterwards.''

Foucault, standing to one side seemingly waiting for any forthcoming orders, had been taking in the conversation thus far as though without interest. But at Zimmerman's words he scowled.

Brecht looked up at the French-Moroccan. ''Amazon, do you have a gun?''

''Why, yes, Señor Brecht. I am your bodyguard, as well as your—butler.''

''Could I see it?''

Frowning now, the other hesitated for a moment but then reached beneath his coat and brought forth a laser pistol. He walked to where Brecht sat and handed it over.

''Careful with that,'' he cautioned. ''Do you understand its workings?''

''No, I don't,'' the Peruvian told him and with that he dropped the gun into his jacket pocket.

''What do you think you are doing?''

All eyes were on Brecht now. He said reasonably, ''I don't want an armed Commie around me. For all I know, the Kremlin might decide that since it didn't have a chance of getting me to tell them where the spaceship is, the best thing would be to liquidate me before somebody else talked me into giving up the secret. And guess who is on the scene to do it?''

''Commie?'' Brett-James queried. ''I say, what in the devil are you talking about, Kraut?''

''The Amazon here is a Commie agent. Last

night he tried to bribe the Kike into getting me to reveal the spaceship's location. The Kike bribes easy."

"That doesn't sound like the Kike," Azikiwe protested.

"The hell it doesn't," Zimmerman said, cheerful still. And then to Brecht, "What do you mean *easy*? A hundred million pseudo-dollars. . . . Each man has his price; I admit that's mine. I like the way the sum rolls around on the tongue."

Foucault was still staring in frustration at the man who had taken his gun. He said indignantly, "I could get that away from you."

Brecht shook his head. "I doubt it. There are five of us here and I suspect the other four are just as anxious not to see me shot as I am. Even our corrupted Kike: You see, he still loves me. The Chink, by the way, knows kempo, so I understand; and the Nigger, judo. You'd have quite a time taking the gang of us. Of course, you're free to try."

The French-Moroccan stayed put. "I suppose you want me to leave."

"Not at all, not at all," Brecht told him. "You make a wonderful Man Friday. We don't have any secrets around here that you can't hear—save my one big one. I just didn't want you trotting around with a gun."

Foucault was furious. He spun on his heel and stomped out of the room.

"By George," Brett-James murmured. "You've hurt his feelings."

Brecht turned back to the others. "Well, since most of you made your play and flubbed it—some conspirators you are—you might as well take off.''

"Take off where?" Zimmerman asked.

"Anywhere you want. Go on back to Israel, or wherever. Nobody's got anything against you. You'll get your pension.''

"The hell with that," Zimmerman said, indignation in his voice. "I'm in this for the duration. There's too much fun and games going on to leave now." He looked about the suite. "Besides, if I'm not going to get my split of the hundred million, the next best thing would be to continue living here." He leered at the two women. "Good booze, good broads . . . and everything.''

Li Ching snorted.

Brett-James said thoughtfully. "Besides, there might be some elements that don't believe that lie test was really true. They might pick up any one of us and twist our arms a bit, don't you know. "I think I'll stick around as well."

"I'm in for the duration too," Azikiwe said. "I'd feel like I was letting the team down if I went back to Africa at this stage.''

"Thanks, Nigger," Brecht said.

Li Ching's eyes were on the floor. She said humbly, "I too will stay, if you will have me. I am ashamed of what I did last night.''

At that point, Mary Lou entered the room, followed by one of the guards carrying her small bag.

"Yawl back already?" Zimmerman said.

"How is your mother, dear?" Azikiwe asked.

"She's all right, thanks," Mary Lou said. She

looked at her lover. "I came back as soon as I could. This must be terribly trying for you. You should see some of the headlines. Why, most people seem to have no conception of what you're talking about, what your motivation is. Many think you should be forced in some manner to reveal where the ship is."

"They'll get around to that," Zimmerman said. "Don't think they won't." He looked directly at Brecht. "There's a lot of different ways to force the information out of you, Kraut. Physical ways, chemical ways."

"I know," Brecht said. "The only reason they haven't already tried is that they can't decide who is to have the privilege. And none of them trusts any of the others."

The guard had put Mary Lou's bag down and left the room. And now Foucault reentered.

He said suavely, "I am happy to see that you have returned so soon, Yawl."

"Those nicknames are used only among we six, Foucault." Brecht brought the laser pistol from his pocket and pointed it at him. "Frisk him, Kike."

Zimmerman's eyebrows went up, but he obeyed. Taking care not to come between the French-Moroccan and the gun, he circled behind him and carefully shook him down. He discovered another laser pistol. "Well, I'll be buggered," he said. "A two-gun man."

"He went to report to his superiors. It would seem they must be right here in this same building, or he wouldn't have gotten back so soon. He simply got himself another gun." Brecht looked at Zimmerman. "You keep that one. I assume you know how to use it."

He turned to Brett-James and handed over the gun he had taken earlier. "And you better have this one. If he turns up with still another, I'll keep that, athough I'd probably shoot my foot off with it."

Azikiwe said, "I can use a laser pistol. I used to have one in Nigeria."

"Some toys you have in Nigeria." Brecht said. "But okay. The next gat the Amazon turns up with goes to you. If he keeps up this pace, soon we'll all be armed."

The French-Moroccan was livid. He stomped out of the room again.

Brett-James was laughing. "I say, I'll wager his superiors give him the works this time."

"Yeah." Zimmerman laughed too. "But I'll bet they don't give him another gun."

Mary Lou slumped down into a chair. "What the devil goes on around here?" she said. "I'm not out of sight of the five of you for more than twenty-four hours and everything happens but the building burning down."

Zimmerman chuckled. "All of us have been approached in attempts to get the location of the extraterrestrial ship from the Boche, one way or another. Evidently he's smarter than he looks; none of us was able to do it. And now that he's on his guard, we've given up. Or, at least, I have. And we've all decided to rally around, don't you know," he grinned at Brett-James, "and see this thing through to whatever end—probably ours."

Brecht looked at Mary Lou questioningly. "How about Yawl?"

"I'm staying too, of course."

"You sure you shouldn't be down in South Carolina with your mother, darling?"

"No. She's quite all right."

"How about some more coffee all around?" Azikiwe said. "Yawl, have you had breakfast?" She rose to her feet, preparatory to going into the dining room.

"Yes, thanks, Nigger." She turned to Brecht, her face worried. "But so far you still haven't told anybody?"

"So far."

Azikiwe came back from the dining room with a coffee pot and six cups in a stack. "The damn coffee's lukewarm," she complained. "Anybody want some?"

"In spite of the hour, I'll have a drink instead," Zimmerman said.

The others took the lukewarm coffee while he went over to the bar and poured himself a Scotch and soda.

"I miss that bastard Amazon," he said suddenly. "I always wanted to be waited on hand and foot, and now, when I finally get someone to do it, the goddamned Boche here drives him off."

"I suspect he'll be back," Brett-James said. "By George, the Soviets must be frantic. They're the only major power that doesn't have a contact on the team."

"I'm their contact," Zimmerman said earnestly,

returning with his drink. "One hundred million pseudo-bucks. How much do you have to pay in tax on that sort of income?"

"You never have to pay income tax on a hundred million pseudo-dollars," Mary Lou explained. "Not here in America. When you have that sort of money, you can hire a flock of tax experts and not pay anything at all. It's an American institution."

"Tut tut, don't be bitter, Yawl," Zimmerman said. "I hate a bitter woman." He looked reflective. "I bitter woman once, and she bit me back."

Brett-James groaned.

Brecht put his coffee cup down and looked around.

"All right, team, now we get down to basics," he began. "I suggest you all reconsider. The real trouble will begin shortly. There's no reason for any of you to be in the line of fire. You didn't start this. I did."

"Oh, I say, old chap, let's not be ridiculous, you know," Brett-James put in. "All for one and one for all and all that rot."

Brecht looked at the Englishman. "They're running around as though their heads were cut off, Your Majesty. But they're going to get organized shortly, and then they'll land on me like a ton of crap. They want that spaceship. They want it so bad they can taste it. So far, everyone who wants it wants if for themselves—exclusively. But even that might end. You might get various mergers, like United America and Common Europe, or the Soviet Complex and the People's Republic of China, or any other combination. The Nigger, for instance, tells me that the Afro-Asian Bloc would like an in. Sooner or later, they're going to lower the boom on me—and those close to me. What happens if they get hold of one of you and stick in the thumbscrews, with me watching. Do you think that under this hypnotic affection thing I could watch you being tortured? I might be able to stick it out if I was the one getting it, but how about if it was Yawl, or the Chink, or the Nigger?''

"Perhaps you had best give up, Boche, I should think," Brett-James said softly. "No man should carry the burdens of the world on his back. Let them do it. Let them work it out, don't you know."

"Yes, I suspect I do know. The world would wind up blown to bits," Brecht said bitterly. "We're savages."

Azikiwe, who had taken the seat next to Mary Lou, spoke up. "What did you think was going to happen when you first dreamed up this idea of keeping the location secret?"

He made a face. "I'm not sure I know. Perhaps that the Reunited Nations would make some sort of supreme effort and become the organization it originally set out to be. Under a real Reunited Nations, perhaps I would eventually have seen fit to give out the information. At least I think I would. I'd really have to trust them first."

"Well," Brett-James said. "I dare say it won't be too long before we find out. According to the news this morning, they are going to begin debating the subject today."

Mary Lou snorted and sipped at her cold coffee. "If it's like the rest of their Reunited Nations debates on anything important, it'll take forever."

And Zimmerman said with unwonted gravity, "Meanwhile, our four powers aren't going to be idle. I'm glad we've got these two laser pistols, at least."

CHAPTER ELEVEN

IN THE DIMLY lit Men's Bar of the Nuovo Italo-American Club, four young men sat about a table in an isolated alcove. They had made sure to pick a spot where they couldn't be heard, and couldn't be approached without warning.

Joseph Nazioni, the eldest of the quartet and their recognized leader, said softly, "It would be the biggest caper of all times." He was a slight man, quick of movement, a bit on the nervous side. His dark good looks, his sharp dark eyes, his beautifully barbered black hair reflected his Italian ancestry. Like the other three, he was perfectly groomed, his suit probably the product of London tailors, rather than the flashier Roman ones.

Luigi Galanti, the youngest, heavyset, said, "But the day of the caper is over, Joe. With the cops as efficient as they are, and the tough laws against carrying guns and so forth, only a jerk would stick his neck out. Besides, those that do try to take a score have their work cut out for them. With almost all business done with universal credit cards, you don't get enough money together in one pile to make it worth swiping."

Rudi Mecholam put in, "I'm inclined to back Luigi. The day of the caper is over. It's a sucker's game. Today we're legitimate—all of the families. Even when we go in for something like gambling, it's legitimate gambling, in Vegas and Reno, or over in the Bahamas or Monte Carlo. Even when we've got interests in the unions, they're legal unions, not any of that waterfront stuff of fifty years ago. We never stick our necks out. The families have got their money tied up in resorts, restaurant chains, hotels, even in banks and securities. We even pay income tax. Hell, my family alone retains twenty lawyers on a full-time basis. We never do anything they could hang a rap on."

Nazioni looked at the last member of the group.

Tolomeo Gallio was the least vocal of the four. His people must have come from Northern Italy; he was comparatively fair and his eyes were blue. He said, "Tell us about it, Joe."

Nazioni looked at each of them, then took a pull at his Scotch. Then he made his pitch. "Rudi and Luigi were right when they said that the caper has become a sucker's game. The day of robbing a bank is over. Sucker stuff. As a result, none of us has a record. None of us has ever even been fingerprinted. We have Ivy League degrees. We're clean. That has its advantages."

"Go on," Gallio said.

"But there's another thing. None of us is prominent in our families. Not one of us has a chance ever to become a Don. Oh, we'll all live well enough. The families take care of their own. But we'll never hit the top."

The others shifted in their chairs. But they nodded.

"This would be the jackpot."

"How big a jackpot?" Galanti said.

Nazioni looked at him and grinned. "What would you say to a billion pseudo-dollars?"

"I'd say you're out of your mind," Gallio said.

"No, I'm not."

"Whoever you got it from would hit you the minute the deal was over."

"No they wouldn't. We'd have it delivered to a bank in Switzerland and divvy it up. Anyway, maybe it'd be best to spend the rest of our lives there; nobody ever gets hit in Switzerland. With a quarter of a billion apiece, we could build houses ass-deep in security and surround ourselves with guards. We'd be able to live as high on the hog as you can get."

"Who's going to give you a billion dollars?" Mecholam muttered. "That's crazy."

"No it's not. In fact, that's peanuts. Maybe we ought to put the guy up in kind of an auction. Let him go to the biggest bidder. What the hell's a billion pseudo-dollars to United America, or a billion rubles to the Soviet Complex? Hell, we could demand it in gold!"

They sat silently for a long time.

Finally, Gallio said, "All right, what's the story? I'm not buying it yet, but let's hear your plan."

"He's in the penthouse of the Reunited Nations Building."

"And shit-deep in guards," Galanti added.

"The guards are all around, but not in the suite

they occupy. They only go inside when something special comes up. He's alone in there with the five other members of the Luna team and one guy who amounts to a butler.''

''Well, how in the hell can we get him out, if there's guards all around?''

Nazioni said very slowly, ''At night, the office rooms directly under the suite are unoccupied. There's only one watchman on the floor. Then we move fast. We cut a hole in the floor right below the bathroom for his room, and go up and snatch him.''

''How do you know where his bathroom is?'' Mecholam demanded.

Nazioni grinned at him. ''I got to one of the maids who helps make up the rooms for this Luna team. She drew me a plan of the suite.''

''Did you say cut a hole in the floor?'' Gallio asked.

''That's right. With a laser. During the day one of us dresses like a workman, takes a ladder up to the floor below and leaves it in a broom closet. At two in the morning, the building is damn near empty—I've cased it. We haul him out to an elevator and take him all the way down to the car pool in the basement. We grab a car and take off.''

''Oh, we do, eh? With all the watchmen taking a shot at us?'' Galanti scoffed.

There's not a person in the world who doesn't know that guy's face. Certainly everybody who works in the Reunited Nations Building knows he's there. They've seen his face in the papers and on TV. They won't shoot. They'd be afraid of nail-

110

ing him. He's the most important guy in the world, which : exactly why he's worth at least a billion."

"Okay," Mecholam conceded. "And then what?"

"Standard procedure for a snatch, the way they pulled them in the old days. We take him to a hideout and then we approach the governments of United America, Common Europe, the Soviet Complex, and the People's Republic of China. Highest bidder gets him."

"Yeah," Gallio said. "And then the other three will jump the country that got him and we'll have an all-out war on our hands. And when this next war starts, even Switzerland will get it."

But Nazioni was shaking his head. "No, because nobody will know who has him. We won't tell them. Each will *suspect* the others, but they won't be sure."

Galanti said musingly, "What do you think will happen to the guy?"

"They'll put him under pressure and, when he breaks, ship him up to the moon to lead them to the spaceship. Not that we give a damn about that. It's no skin off our backs."

"Well," Mecholam said, "I hope this country is top bidder. I'd rather our scientists had it than anybody else."

"You turning patriotic on us?" Nazioni laughed. He signaled the waiter for another round.

Jean Hippolyte Foucault was on the carpet. His too-handsome face was apprehensive.

The very efficient-looking type behind the desk

said, "I am Colonel Alexander Grozny. I have been sent from Moscow. I am now in command of this operation."

"Yes, Comrade Colonel."

"Don't call me comrade, you fouled-up mess. I should have you liquidated."

"Yes, Colonel."

"If I understand the reports correctly—how anyone could understand them is a mystery to me—you were infiltrated into the very quarters of these cosmonauts, or whatever they call them."

"Astronauts, in United America, Colonel. They call themselves Lunatics, I believe, among themselves."

"Keep your stupid mouth shut until I ask you to open it. Now then, in your words, what happened? You have no idea of the difficulties we had smuggling you into their inner circle. As chance would have it, we had no representatives of the Soviet Complex on this Luna team. Even the People's Republic was respresented, but not us. We simply had to get someone in who could report to us. And we got you."

"Yes, Comrade Colonel," Foucault said miserably.

"All right. Tell me what has happened?"

"I met them all and I was on as friendly terms as possible with them. I believe I can say I was doing very well in this regard, though they are a close-knit group. To attempt to learn the location of the spacecraft from beyond I approached the one who seemed the most easygoing, possibly the most corruptible. He is an Israeli and hence unaligned."

"Max Zimmerman, the psychiatrist?" the KGB man said, looking down at a report on the desk.

"Yes. I offered him a hundred million pseudo-dollars if he would reveal the location of the spaceship."

"Where did you expect to acquire that sum?"

"I thought it would be forthcoming if the information was revealed."

The KGB man said sourly, "It probably would have been . . . if only to cement the bargain. Or any other astronomical amount. And then what happened?"

"It would seem that Werner Brecht is suspicious to the point of neurosis, even of these most immediate friends of his. Also, he has an absolute fixation so far as not revealing the location of the extraterrestrial craft is concerned. The hundred million pseudo-dollars did not interest him."

The colonel regarded his underling for a long moment. "What motivates him? He comes from a capitalist country. The sum offered is fantastic."

Foucault said, "He is what the Americans call a bleeding heart. In short, an idealist, in his own eyes. Perhaps we could offer him still more."

The colonel was contemptuous. "There is no more. Anyone who would reject a hundred million Yankee pseudo-dollars would reject their whole treasury." He paused. "And the others?"

"From the little I have seen of them, I would say that Max Zimmerman is, within reason, an opportunist and cynic. From what he has said to the others, and to me, he expects this whole thing to result in world catastrophe whatever happens. And he doesn't mind living out the rest of whatever existence remains in the utmost luxury, such as a hundred million pseudo-dollars, or half of it, represents. But then, he is also somewhat devious. I cannot figure him out. He is, after all, a goddamned Jew.''

''Ummm. And the rest?''

''The Nigerian woman, Doctor Awolowo, is also of an unaligned nation, but seemingly is in accord with Brecht. She is strong and I doubt if she would bend even under extreme pressure.''

Colonel Grozny said wryly, ''You would be surprised what pressures we can bring to bear. I could not stand them myself, and most certainly you couldn't.''

''Yes, Comrade Colonel.''

''Go on.''

''The American, Mary Lou Pickett, is probably the weakest. And she is the closest to Brecht, being his mistress.''

''We know about her. She supposedly left the Reunited Nations Building penthouse to go to her ailing mother in South Carolina but was, instead, taken to the Octagon. We were unable to discover what took place there. Our organization here in America needs some shaking up.''

''Yes, Comrade Colonel.''

The other looked at him in disgust. ''All right, finish up.''

''Brett-James, who was their communications officer on Luna, is a British subject. I suppose that he is loyal to the British throne, being of the old aristocratic, reactionary school, and that he attempted, unsuccessfully, to get Brecht to reveal the location of the spaceship to Common Europe."

"Is there any possible manner of getting to him?"

"I doubt it."

"I suppose there is no purpose in asking about the confounded Chinese?"

"No, Comrade Colonel. She is a Party member and, I gather, dedicated. The rest of them, including Brecht, are very fond of her."

"I understand you have been exposed by this Werner Brecht."

"Yes."

"And he took two weapons from you, you fool."

"I could not avoid it."

"But he hasn't taken measures to expel you from the suite." The KGB man's voice was puzzled.

The French-Moroccan shook his head. "No. I suspect he reasons that it is better to have a known enemy around rather than an unknown. If I was replaced as their majordomo, he wouldn't know who that new person represented."

"I see. Very well. I have, only last night, been in conference with Number One himself and the Central Committee. It has been decided that if it is absolutely impossible for us to extract the information involving the location of the spaceship, that no one else must either. They are opposed not only to turning the spacecraft over to the Reunited Nations, but also to a consortium of the nations with space programs. We either get it exclusively, or no one gets it."

"Yes, Comrade Colonel." There was apprehension in Foucault's eyes. He thought he knew what was coming.

"Very well. You will return to their quarters but keep in touch with me hourly, by tight beam. They have taken two laser pistols from you; you will now be supplied with a miniature weapon which they will not detect in your clothing. If ordered, you will liquidate this Werner Brecht."

"I . . . I do not think I would have the opportunity, Comrade Colonel. The others seem firmly committed to him. Two of them are now armed. The rest seem to be excellent physical specimens, as obviously all Luna teams must be, and also familiar with hand-to-hand combat such as judo."

On the face of it the French-Moroccan was not the most aggressive underground agent in the world. The colonel looked at him coldly. "This is not my problem, *Comrade* Foucault. If, in the old days, a dedicated comrade was able to get through the defenses of the counter-revolutionist Trotsky in Mexico and assassinate him, I assume your own dedication is not the less."

Colonel Alexander Grozny added, almost to himself, "There is another aspect. If we learn where the space vessel is, then it will be imperative to liquidate Brecht immediately so that he will not be able to tell anyone else. That task very possibly would descend upon you. On the other hand, if it is necessary to take him to Luna so that he can lead us to the vessel, then we will finish him off there."

CHAPTER TWELVE

WHEN KINGSLEY BRETT-JAMES and Azikiwe Awolowo entered the living room on the following morning, Max Zimmerman and Li Ching were already at the TV set.

"What's up Kike?" the Englishman said.

Zimmerman grinned at him. "More or less what was to be expected. All sorts of speeches, all sorts of resolutions—none of which pass."

Li Ching said, "India proposed that the Kraut turn over the location of the extraterrestrial ship to the Reunited Nations and that it be investigated by the organization as a whole. Both the Soviet Complex and China then announced that even if the Reunited Nations were able to get together sufficiently to pass such a resolution in the General Assembly, they would veto it. Common Europe has made no announcements, but it is obvious they feel the same way."

Zimmerman added, "The Soviets have a cute little twist. They think they ought to get first dibs on the spaceship in view of the fact that they were the first Earth power to go into space."

Li Ching said, "United America has made just as ridiculous a claim: since they were the first to put a man on the moon, they should take over the ship."

Brett-James looked at her. "And what claim does the government of the People's Republic make, old thing?"

She flushed ever so slightly. "Thus far, none, nor has Common Europe."

"They'll both came up with something, I should think."

Zimmerman had turned back to the set. Somebody else was giving another boring speech.

He said, even as he fiddled with the set to get another channel, "Where in the devil are the Kraut and Yawl? They're usually up and around by this time."

"Probably enjoying an extra roll in the hay, I shouldn't wonder," Brett-James said. "After all, the girl was gone a full twenty-four hours. The Kraut will have to catch up."

Zimmerman said to Azikiwe, "That outfit you want to join up with is having a field day, Nigger."

"What outfit?"

"That World Government League. Evidently they're showing more strength than anyone knew they had. All sorts of speeches on both TV and radio; parades in their favor in Sweden, Denmark, Argentina, India, and Japan. Demonstrations against the four space powers who continue to ignore the League, and demands for immediate

118

amalgamation of all countries into one world state. They're really sounding off.''

Azikiwe was impressed. "I still think they make more sense than anyone else. All the heat going on now is the result of the world being split up into a hundred and fifty different nations, most of whom would like a private crack at the spaceship. I wonder what the Kraut thinks about the League. If he came out in their favor, it would swing a lot of clout.''

Foucault entered and bid them all good morning.

Brett-James looked at Zimmerman. "I say, do you think we ought to shake him down again?''

The Israeli looked at the French-Moroccan, then shook his head. "He's not too sharp, or he wouldn't have let the Boche get his first two guns, but I doubt if he's silly enough to contribute another.''

Foucault looked indignant for just a moment. "Breakfast is ready to be served. Haven't Ms. Pickett and Doctor Brecht arisen as yet?''

"Rather obviously not," Brett-James said, coming to his feet. "Why don't you go and knock?''

"Yes sir." Foucault headed for the door of the bedroom. While the others filed into the dining room and headed for the buffet with its covered dishes of eggs in several styles, bacon, ham, sausage, and kidneys, he knocked, at first discreetly, and then more sharply, without result.

At the entrance to the dining room he announced, "They don't respond.''

"That's funny. They're both good chompers, usually right up in front when it comes to break-

119

fast." Zimmerman put down the plate of shirred eggs. "I'll give them a call," he said.

He went into the living room and down the short hall leading to the bedrooms. He banged on the door so loudly the others could hear him in the dining room. "Hey, Kraut, Yawl, come on to breakfast."

He pounded again. "Werner!"

Brett-James put his own plate down hurriedly and strode to Zimmerman's side.

"Something's wrong, Kingsley!" He stood back a ways and butted his shoulder against the door as the others were coming up. It failed to give.

"What's going on?" Azikiwe asked, worry in her voice.

"I say, I'll give you a hand, old chap," Brett-James offered.

Together they exerted their full weight and after three tries the door crashed inward, the lock splintering.

Li Ching said, "They never keep the door locked."

Zimmerman and Brett-James dashed inside. The lights were out and heavy curtains drawn over the windows. The Israeli flicked the light switch.

One bed was empty, the other held a wide-eyed Mary Lou Pickett, her mouth efficiently taped shut.

Brett-James hurried to her bed and threw back the covers. Her hands and feet were bound with what looked like old-fashioned clothesline. He pulled the tape from her mouth.

"Where's Werner?" Zimmerman snapped.

"Bathroom. They came out of the bathroom.

They went back, taking him with them. There were four of them."

Zimmerman let Brett-James take over with the ropes and hurried to the king-size bathroom, Li Ching and Azikiwe right behind, Foucault bringing up the rear.

In almost the exact center of the room was a round hole about the diameter of a sewer manhole. They could stare down to the office below. The ladder was still in place.

Foucault turned and darted from the room.

"Stop him!" Zimmerman snapped, racing after him, the others following.

Brett-James shook his head. "We can't, unless we're willing to shoot him. We aren't, I shouldn't think."

Mary Lou was sitting up now, rubbing her arms.

"What time did they grab him?" Zimmerman demanded of her.

"It must have been about two o'clock," she said weakly. "They just came walking in from the bathroom, as businesslike as could be."

"Who were they?" Zimmerman insisted.

"I . . . I don't know, Max. And I don't think Werner did, either. Three of them were rather dark, possibly Spanish. The other was somewhat lighter."

"What language did they speak?"

"English."

"No accent?"

"Not that I caught. But they didn't talk much at all. They were very efficient, very quick. They knew exactly what they were doing."

Brett-James said, "Could they have been Russians, or any other race within the Soviet Complex?"

"Not Russian, I wouldn't think, but maybe Bulgarians or Rumanians or something."

Li Ching said, "They certainly weren't Chinese."

"No," Mary Lou agreed, getting her legs over the side of the bed. "They couldn't have been Chinese."

Zimmerman said sourly, "But they could have been somebody working for the People's Republic."

"My country does not do such things," Li Ching said indignantly.

"And I'm the Queen of Zebovia," Zimmerman growled. "Damn it, it could have been just about anybody."

For some reason not spoken about, but accepted by all, he had taken over the leadership of the team, a leadership that had formerly been held by Werner Brecht, though somewhat loosely.

Zimmerman grimaced with frustration. "We've got to get out of here immediately if we're going to do the Kraut any good. That damned French-Moroccan is getting the word out to his people right this minute. Before we know it, we're going to be under house detention."

"Help him how?" Mary Lou wailed. "We don't know where he is, or who has him, or even why."

"We know why," Brett-James said. "And I'm working on figuring out a manner in which it's possible to find out where he is." He looked at Zimmerman. "What's the drill, old chap?"

Zimmerman said, "We couldn't get past the guards outside in a million years. They'd want to start phoning, to get permission from everybody and his cousin. No. We'll have to leave the same way the kidnappers did. Down the ladder. Come on. We'll be getting invaded any minute. Your Majesty, help Mary Lou—she's still stiff. I'll go first and hold the ladder down below."

He went down, then looked up anxiously as first Li Ching, then Azikiwe, then Brett-James steadying Mary Lou above him, scrambled after him.

They were in a lengthy office room filled with IBM computers and other office equipment unknown to any of them. At this time of the morning, none of the office staff had yet made an appearance. Scattered about the floor was the debris from the nighttime caper.

"Must have used a laser," Zimmerman muttered in disgust. "Why didn't the stupid Reunited Nations security people have a guard posted down here?"

"By George, it evidently never occured to them, don't you know," Brett-James said, equally disgusted. "What now?"

"I suspect they must have used a service elevator and probably took it all the way down to the basements. Come on." Zimmerman led the way. Azikiwe brought up the rear with Mary Lou, who was still having a bit of trouble walking. Both Brett-James and Zimmerman carried laser pistols and required their hands free for any difficulties they might encounter.

In the corridor outside the office, they discovered a uniformed watchman, dead.

"These boys mean business," Zimmerman said. "Keep it in mind: they're playing for keeps."

They searched around, finally found the service elevator. It was slow, and the building a tall one. The descent from the floor below the penthouse to the basement levels took a long time.

Zimmerman looked serious. "Okay, let's get down to the old nitty-gritty, as the expression goes. Are we on the side of the Kraut, or are we being nationalistic? You, Yawl, are you waving that red, white and blue? Your Majesty, are you fundamentally a loyal subject of the King? I'm not forgetting the time the Kraut brought you in from the surface when the sharp rock cut your airline——"

"Oh, screw you, Kike," Azikiwe said angrily. "You know damn well we're all in. Drop the bullshit, and let's get talking practically. I still haven't the vaguest idea of how we're going to find Werner."

"Of course the only thing that counts is finding the Kraut," Li Ching put in.

"Oh," Zimmerman mocked, "so you're calling him the Kraut again, eh, Chink?"

Li Ching said softly, "He will always be the Kraut to me." And then she added caustically, "And you'll always be the Kike, you Kike."

"Obviously," he laughed warmly.

"Jolly well told," said Brett-James.

Zimmerman looked at him. "Jolly well told? Next you'll be saying *pip, pip*. Jesus! No wonder Israel had so much trouble with you people in the old days."

They reached the basement level and emerged from the service elevator into the gigantic car pool. At this time of the day it was beginning to bustle; a multitude of cars were darting every which way.

Zimmerman stopped a coverall-clad attendant. "Listen, would there be any way of finding out whether five men left this place about two o'clock this morning?"

The other looked at him scornfully. "How the hell would I know? I wasn't on duty. There's not much traffic then, but I doubt if anybody would have noticed them anyway. There's over a thousand vehicles in this park." He walked away.

Zimmerman yelled after him, "Hey, where do we rent a car?"

The attendant pointed. "Over there."

"Come on," Zimmerman said to the others. "Anybody got a universal credit card? Mine lapsed while I was on the moon."

"I have," Brett-James offered. "I had mine renewed while I was at the Embassy."

Renting a car couldn't have been easier. The clerk evidently failed to recognize them. After all it was Brecht's face that had been plastered all over the news media.

Zimmerman took the wheel, piloting on manual until they reached the ramp and departed the building, and were heading down the boulevard.

"But where are we going?" Mary Lou asked. The three women were seated in the back of the hover limousine they had selected, Brett-James up in front with Zimmerman.

"Spaceport."

"Spaceport!" Azikiwe echoed. "I thought we were going to look for the Kraut, Max. I don't know where to begin, but offhand I'd think the spaceport would be about the last place."

"I didn't mean that he'd be there, but that's our first stop. Why? Well, are any of you still wearing your electronic I.D. tags—you know, the ones we used up on Luna?"

"Why . . . why, yes," Mary Lou said, it beginning to dawn on her. "I kept it on, sort of like a souvenir of my Luna tour of duty."

It turned out that all of them were still wearing their I.D. tags about their necks.

Zimmerman spoke to Mary Lou. "You sleep with the Boche. Did he have his on?"

Her eyes rounded. "Now that you mention it . . ."

"Good," he said. "What we need now is a direction finder. One small enough to be portable."

"Right," Brett-James assented. "I had the same idea, when I said I thought it possible to find him."

At the spaceport, they parked in the official lot and made their way to the administration building of the Ozma Project Department.

"I hope to hell nobody wonders what we're doing here," Zimmerman muttered. "If anybody asks, our story is that we're here to check up on the reorientation course we were supposed to go through after a Luna tour."

Brett-James said, "I say, I do hope that Harlan Jones is on duty."

"Why?" Li Ching asked him.

"Because he owes me a few favors. He's ugly

126

as a monkey but when he came over to London about a year ago, I set him up with some very tasty dishes."

"You lecherous cad." Azikiwe made a face. "We'll go into that later."

He put one hand over his heart and said innocently, "But that was before I met you, Nigger."

They made their way to the Communications Section and though Harlan Jones wasn't on duty, he was on standby in one of the bedrooms connected with the Department. Brett-James got directions.

The others remained in a nearby waiting room downing coffee and sweet rolls while the Englishman went about the business of acquiring a directional finder of the type used with their electronic I.D. tags.

Brett-James returned in under half an hour, bearing what looked like a rather large portable radio.

He grinned. "I had to twist his arm a little. He was a bit suspicious about my wanting this. But here we are—brand new, right out of stock."

"Let's get going," Zimmerman said. "The range of that damn thing isn't infinite, and we don't want them to get too far away."

As soon as they were back in the limousine, Brett-James pulled the antenna out and opened the side of the direction finder so that he could get at the switches, dials, and knobs. "Does anybody know the Kraut's I.D. number?"

Mary Lou said promptly, "H-420."

Brett-James nodded. He set one of the dials and flicked a switch. The antenna slowly turned.

"Here we go," he muttered, when the small arrow mounted on it settled down.

Zimmerman started up the vehicle. "I'm not checked out on that gadget," he said. "Have you any idea of how far off he is?"

"About twenty kilometers, I shouldn't wonder."

"So," the Israeli said with satisfaction, "they brought him out on this side of the city. It'll make finding him a damn sight quicker."

"It would seem so. He's somewhere in the country, I should say, Kike. We would have had our work cut out finding him in the center of Greater Washington, even with this device."

From time to time, as they proceeded, Brett-James fiddled with his dials. Since they had to keep to the roads, they couldn't follow the arrow as the bird flies, but slowly they zeroed in on the area indicated.

Mary Lou said suddenly, "What do we do when we get there? Those men were all armed."

CHAPTER THIRTEEN

NOBODY ANSWERED her.

Brett-James said, more excitement in his voice than was his wont, "I think that's it, by George! That rather large house up on the hill."

Zimmerman came to a halt immediately and the five of them contemplated the building.

"I wouldn't be surprised," Li Ching said. "The way it's situated, anyone approaching can be seen. It's an ideal setting for a hideout."

Zimmerman asked Brett-James, "Have you had any experience in house-to-house fighting, door-to-door combat? You know, when you're flushing out the enemy who's gone to ground in a building and has probably fortified it."

The Englishman looked a bit startled. "Well, no, old chap. I was in the air force before I got into the space force, you know."

Zimmerman took a deep breath. "Well, this is how it works. Speed is everything. You've got to keep on the move. You break in fast, and you come in shooting. You shoot at anything that moves. We're at a disadvantage here, because the Kraut is in there too and we don't want to cut him down. But there's at least four men in there with him and they're all armed. Don't hesitate for a minute, and don't try to take prisoners. They're kidnappers, and a kidnapper is a potential killer. In fact, they've already killed one man. Shoot first.''

''I say . . .'' Brett-James began.

''This is what we'll do. The front door is undoubtedly guarded. It will also be the strongest door, and I doubt if we'd have the chance to cut it open with our guns before they were prepared for us. What we'll do is slam up that hill as fast as this thing will take us, and then around to the back. The back door is usually the weakest one in a house. You blast the lock away and then stand to one side and I'll rush in and pop to the right—shooting, if anyone's there. Then you pop in behind me and jump to the left.''

''And then?''

''And then we play it by ear,'' Zimmerman said. ''They nabbed the Boche at two o'clock. They were probably up all night. It's now well past noon. Most likely some of them will be sleeping.''

''What do we three do?'' Azikiwe asked.

''The moment I'm out of the car, you scramble up here to the driver's seat and be all set to go. We might have to come out shooting and possibly one of us, or the Kraut, will have taken a hit. As soon as we get back into the car, move like a bat out of hell. If we don't come out within a few minutes, take off anyway, particularly if you come under fire. Return to this spot and get on the car phone and call the police and anybody else you can think of."

"I'm going in too," Mary Lou said. "He's my man."

"Like hell you are," Zimmerman told her. "We don't want to have to be worrying about you. If we had another gun, I'd say okay to Azikiwe, since she says she can handle a laser pistol. Since we haven't, she stays out here too."

"My father was a Nigerian paramount chief, and I was raised in a military atmosphere. I'm going in too. Mary Lou or Li Ching can drive the car."

"I am a member of the Party and three of my grandparents were on the Long March with Chairman Mao. I would be disgraced if I did not do all I could for my comrades. Besides, I know kempo. I'm going in too."

"What is this, a picnic?" Zimmerman protested. "Those men are armed. And desperate. Now shut up and obey orders."

Nothing went the way Max Zimmerman had planned it. Absolutely nothing.

They sped up the hill dramatically. Since it was a hover car, they were able to ignore the driveway and stuck to the lawns. They whipped around the house and the Israeli slammed on the brakes. He and Brett-James zipped out of the vehicle on either side, laser pistols in hand, and raced for the back porch.

The Englishman had brought up his gun to blast the lock off the door when they noticed it was slightly ajar.

Zimmerman gestured for his companion to stand to one side. He slammed the door open and jumped in and to the right, his gun ready at chest level.

He was in the kitchen, and there was no one else there.

Brett-James rushed in and flew to the left, as ordered. He was also taken aback to find no one to shoot at.

"What now?" he whispered.

Zimmerman was disconcerted. He could hear no sound in the house. Someone should have heard the banging of the door, at least, and come to investigate.

He gestured toward the interior of the house, then moved quietly toward the kitchen door.

He stood to one side and opened it slightly to peer through. There was no one in the hall beyond. Five doors opened off it, two at each side and one at the end. All but one were closed.

When they reached the first door, Zimmerman gestured to Brett-James to cover the others. He twisted the knob, flung open the door, and bounded inside.

He was back in the hall a split second later. "Empty bedroom," he whispered. Then, "Are you sure this is the house that he's in?"

Brett-James merely nodded.

They crossed the hall and repeated their performance, with the same result.

The next door was the one that was open. Zimmerman cautiously peered in.

"Jesus Christ," he muttered softly.

Werner Brecht was spread-eagled on the bed.

On both wrists were old-fashioned handcuffs attached to the steel springs of the bed. He wasn't gagged. His eyes widened at their entrance.

While Brett-James carefully burnt through the steel manacles with his laser ray, Zimmerman bent down so that his lips were near Brecht's ear and whispered, "Where are they?"

Brecht whispered back, "I think one of them left in the car. I heard it start up about a half hour ago. I think the other three are in the front of the house, in the living room. They're armed, Kike."

He was free now, though the handcuffs were still about his wrists like bracelets.

Zimmerman shook his head. "I wonder why they didn't spot us when we drove up the hill. Lucky for us, otherwise they'd be in action by now. Well, one thing's for sure: when we start down that hill again, we'll be sitting ducks. We've got to finish them off. You stay here, Kraut. Better still, go on out and back and get into the car with the women. You're not armed."

"I'm coming," Brecht whispered back.

Zimmerman rolled his eyes upward in protest but they had no time to argue.

They tiptoed down the hall toward the door at the far end. The Israeli motioned Brecht to open it.

The two armed men rushed in, guns at the ready.

A table held cards and poker chips. The chairs knocked to the floor in their haste to rise, three men were standing, wide-eyed, staring in the direction of the French windows that had just banged open to allow Azikiwe Awolowo to come flying into the room. She went for the one nearest the window, going into the twenty-second Kata and screaming, "*ZUT!*" In an automatic defensive reaction, the enemy threw a left punch at her. She rushed in quickly with her left hand, came up and under the other's armpit and shoved him to the right with his arm held high. Now she was behind him. She jumped up and with her right foot kicked him heavily in the kidney. He groaned and fell forward.

The other two women had not been inactive during the performance.

Li Ching had come in running, straight for the one in the middle. Even as he desperately reached for his gun, she left the floor completely; one of her feet lanced into his solar plexus, the other into his groin. He shrieked in agony and clutched his scrotum.

The other had better luck, being on the far side of the table from the invading women. He had his gun out by the time Mary Lou had begun to round the furniture. The fallen chairs impeded her. The man wasn't slow. The gun came up fast.

Azikiwe had taken the time to kick her man in the side of the head, by way of insurance that he wouldn't get back into the action.

Li Ching, seeing the situation out of the corner of her eye, moved quickly in the direction of the gunman. But she was too late.

Zimmerman cut the man down with his laser pistol from the doorway.

Brett-James murmured, "I say, where did *you* people come from?"

Mary Lou stared down at the dead man. "We

. . . we got worried when you didn't come back and we didn't hear any sounds of a fight. We circled around the house and peeked in the windows and saw these three nonchalantly playing cards. So we thought we had better come in and help you fellows out, whatever you were doing."

Brecht shook his head in wonder. Zimmerman and Brett-James reversed their pistols and slugged the two fallen but still conscious men over the head.

"What did you think you were going to do to him when you came charging around the table?" Brecht asked Mary Lou.

"I was going to use my left hook on him."

While the other two women were brushing their pant suits clean, Zimmerman looked around at the carnage.

"We better get out of here," he said. "We know of at least one more of them and he might come back with friends." He added, "Take their guns."

They netted another laser pistol, a .44 Magnum, and, of all things, an old-time Luger. Brecht didn't understand the workings of the laser, so he took the .44 Magnum. Azikiwe took the laser and Li Ching, who had had military training on the commune on which she had been brought up, got the Luger. Only Mary Lou remained unarmed.

Brecht searched the men for the keys to his handcuffs. In moments he had the remnants of the manacles off his wrists.

Zimmerman looked down at the corpse, then at the other two. "We ought to finish them off," he muttered. "Just to play safe."

135

"No," Brecht said.

"They killed one of the watchmen in the Reunited Nations Building."

"I know. I saw it. But there's been too much violence already. Let's just get out of here."

They retraced their path through the house and exited by the kitchen door. They piled into the car, the three men in the front, the girls in the rear seat. Azikiwe kept a lookout through the rear window.

Brecht asked, "How'd you find me, and especially so soon?"

Brett-James told him.

"I'll be damned! I'd forgotten I was wearing it."

Zimmerman was driving. "Who were they?" he asked. "Soviets, American, Common——"

Brecht was shaking his head. "It was an old-fashioned kidnapping. Those guys were the Mafia, or Cosa Nostra, the Syndicate, the Mob—whatever they used to call them. If I got the story right, they were thinking of charging some enormous amount for me from the highest bidder."

Mary Lou said, "It would have been the biggest kidnapping of all time."

"Well, the damn fools didn't know their business. Imagine sitting around playing cards rather than guarding the house," Zimmerman muttered.

"They were supremely confident," Brecht said. "Everything they had planned went off like clockwork. They zigzagged all over the countryside before finally going to that house. Nobody was following. They were sure that they had it made. The one who left had gone off to make the preliminary arrangements to get in touch with the four space powers and offer them my fair body. By the way, where are we going now?''

''Where *can* we go?'' Brett-James said. ''Back to the Reunited Nations Building, I should say.''

Li Ching said unhappily, ''This is just the first attempt on the Kraut. There will be others.''

''Yes, there will be others. And the next one might not be of this type. These people had to keep you alive for their purposes. The next one might be a pure and simple assassination.''

''Such as by whom?'' Brett-James asked.

''Such as some religious crackpot. Somebody possibly willing to give his life in order to suppress this blasphemer. It's hard to defend yourself against a man who is willing to die. There are others . . . those people interested in political economy are all out against the space programs. They think the money and scientific effort should be spent here on Earth relieving poverty and so forth. If the Kraut ever reveals the location of that extraterrestrial ship, there's a good chance the expenditures for space exploration will increase tenfold. For that matter,'' the Nigerian continued, ''it could be some government, or governments, that would be left out, either one of the nations without a space program, or possibly one of those with one who felt they had no chance to get an exclusive.''

Zimmerman said, ''The People's Republic, for instance.''

Li Ching flared, ''China does not commit assassinations.''

Zimmerman said very softly, ''Chink, all countries will commit assassination, or just about anything else, if it is felt to be necessary enough. Offhand, I can't think of an exception in history."

"Look here, this is a fascinating conversation, very cheering, but I haven't eaten since dinner last night. What do you say we stop at one of the automated cafeterias along the route here and get a sandwich or something?"

Brett-James said, "You might be recognized, Brecht."

"I suspect we could find one practically empty at this time of day."

Mary Lou said, "I could go in first and case the joint. If it's empty, or if there's some sort of alcove, then we can all go in."

They were speeding along the highway in the direction of the city.

Azikiwe asked, "Why not wait until we get back to the Reunited Nations Building?"

Brecht replied, "Because when we do we're going to be ass-deep in newspapermen and everybody else, and we won't get a chance to eat."

Brett-James said, "There's one now, and no cars are parked in front."

Zimmerman pulled up and Mary Lou got out and went into the roadside auto-cafeteria. She came out shortly and reported, "Nobody inside at all."

They entered. Just to be sure, they selected the most remote table in the restaurant and Brecht sat so that his back faced the other tables.

Before he could sit down, Mary Lou put her arms around him. "Darling . . . you have no idea how relieved I am to have you back."

He kissed her, smiling. "Thanks, Yawl. It's a bit relieving to me, as well."

They scanned the menus set into the table tops.

Zimmerman said sourly, "Do you think that food will ever come back?"

"I say, what in the hell do you expect, old chap—pastrami?"

"Pastrami, ah," Zimmerman said wistfully. "I guess I'll have this whaleburger. Imagine them herding those poor whales now as though they were cows."

"I think I'll have the pseudo-shrimp," Azikiwe sighed. "Does anybody remember when they had real shrimp last?"

"At twenty pseudo-dollars a serving?" Brecht grunted.

When they had all punched their orders, they sat back almost contentedly, their ordeal behind them. Then Li Ching said, "Somebody mentioned a while back that the only place to go is the Re-united Nations Building penthouse. But is it? The Kraut is a sitting duck there. I do not admit that the People's Republic would attempt his life, under any circumstances, but there are all of the others."

Brett-James looked at her. "Chink, Chink . . . I say, let's not be silly. Where else could we go? At least in the penthouse we have guards."

"Yes," Azikiwe said. "And one of them might be the potential assassin. People have been assassinated by their guards before. Or how about somebody posing as a newspaper photographer with a concealed gun in his camera?"

"Jesus Christ," Zimmerman said accusingly to

Brecht, "why in the hell did you ever find that damn thing?"

"Not on purpose," Brecht told him wearily.

Brett-James said, even as the table top began to descend to bring up their orders, "Well, all I can say, my dear chap, is when you did you should have taken a quick pee on it and then collapsed that shelf over it and never told anybody."

Mary Lou said glumly, "And then some day the extraterrestrials would come back and we wouldn't be prepared for them. We wouldn't even know they existed."

Brecht stood. "Pardon me for a moment. Those characters not only didn't give a damn about my eating, but about other bodily functions either."

"Hurry back," Zimmerman said, reaching for the dishes he had ordered.

When he was gone, the five of them looked at each other.

Azikiwe said, "Somebody's going to get to him. We've been back no time at all, and look—the Soviets worked the Amazon into our suite, and then the Mafia turned up. It's only been a matter of hours, and each of us, except Mary Lou, has been approached with a scheme to wriggle the secret out of him."

"We can't take him back to that place," Mary Lou said.

Zimmerman picked up his knife and fork. "And where can we take him, Yawl?"

Brett-James said, "Maybe out of the country, somewhere."

"Where?" Li Ching said. "There's no place in the whole world where he's safe. How can you hide out in this age? You need your universal credit card to eat, to sleep, for transportation—for everything. And we're as vulnerable as he is. That is, they'd track him down through us if we tried to hide him out. We could hardly breath without our credit cards."

"Where in the hell is he?" Brett-James said suddenly.

Li Ching looked at him. "Why, he's in the men's room."

"Doing what? Taking a bath, by George?" The Englishman tossed his napkin to the table and left.

They stared after him.

He returned in moments, opened his hand, and showed them its contents. He was extremely upset.

"His electronic I.D. tag," he said. "Somebody's got to him again."

CHAPTER FOURTEEN

THEY SPENT THE next half hour scouring the
neighborhood, completely without results. There
was no sign of Werner Brecht whatsoever. Whoever had abducted him this time had managed to
remove him without a trace. There wasn't even a
sign of a struggle in the men's room.

Had they been followed here? Azikiwe swore
that they hadn't, for she had kept watch at all
times through the rear window. But there seemed
to be no other answer to the dilemmá.

Was it the Mafia again? If so, it had to be
another contingent. The three that they had left at
the house were certainly in no condition to take
up the pursuit, and didn't even have a car at their
disposal.

More likely it was some other element interested in the possession of the Peruvian. Mary
Lou had a thoughtful look on her face.

Heavy-hearted, they finally gave up and returned to the Reunited Nations Building. They left

the hover limousine in the basement parking pool and took the elevator up to the penthouse.

There they ran into complete confusion. It seemed that as soon as Foucault had discovered through Colonel Grozny that the Soviet Complex had had nothing to do with the disappearance of Werner Brecht, he had immediately called in the guards and also phoned Director Nilsson Vogel, who promptly hit the ceiling.

By the time the former Luna team arrived, the suite and reception room and the halls were all jam-packed with newspapermen, TV reporters, and technicians. It was a madhouse.

They were interviewed in private by the Director of the Ozma Department, by representatives from the Reunited Nations, and by the same four representatives of the space powers they had met earlier.

They told the story as completely as they could and were then questioned for hours on every phase of it. Their questioners were incredulous. From time to time they eyed each other suspiciously.

At long last, the news media were allowed to enter and the questioning began all over again. They were still at it when night fell, including appearances on TV.

Within hours, the world went mad with the news.

Who had Werner Brecht?

Everybody accused everybody else.

The World Government League intensified its "World Union Now" program: *End War and Prepare for the Extraterrestrials!*

United America, the Soviet Complex, and Common Europe each immediately dispatched two craft to Luna; the People's Republic of China sent one. Each craft contained vehicles approximately the same as the one Brecht had utilized when he found the spaceship. The all but hopeless search was on.

And those who were in charge of conducting it swore mightily at the short-tempered Director of the Ozma Department who had stomped out of his interview with Brecht before asking a wider variety of questions. They didn't even have a compass direction!

All they really knew was that Brecht had said it was about five or six miles from the Luna Hilton as the crow flies, and about ten miles the way a Luna vehicle crawls. All they could do was draw a circle around the Luna Hilton with a diameter of six miles and start looking. It resulted in a fantastically vast area of the broken Luna surface to be searched.

At first it was hoped that they would be able to backtrack the route his vehicle had taken, but they were soon disillusioned on that score. Thousands of tracks crisscrossed the area, made during the period that the Luna Radio Interferometer Observatory and the Luna Hilton and other auxiliary buildings were being constructed. There was no distinguishing his tracks from any of the others.

They pretended, the different search teams, to be on a friendly, cooperative basis, but everyone knew they were only pretending. At least they

were sure of *one* thing: none of them had Werner Brecht; because none of them had the spacecraft.

It was a hopeless search, but no one could afford to give up.

There came a knock at the door of the small room in which he sat reading a newspaper at the table. Werner Brecht looked up, scowling. He didn't like it; he wasn'f expecting anyone at this time. In fact, he wasn't expecting anyone until the following day, with his weekly supplies. However, he stood up, went over and unlocked the door.

Mary Lou Pickett said brightly, "Hello, darling."

He stared at her. He couldn't have been more surprised if she had levitated through a window instead of simply walking in the door. Finally he got out, "How in the hell did you locate me?"

He closed the door behind her and locked it. She put her arms around his neck and kissed him briefly.

"Oh, that was no problem. I'm not as stupid as I look, darling. You see, I was beginning to smell a rat almost from the beginning. Parts of your story don't hold up very well."

"Such as. . . ?" He disengaged her arms and frowned at her.

She smiled innocently at him and said, "Such as the spaceship being under that ledge. How in the world could it ever land on the moon and then move horizonally to a point under a ledge?"

"How did you find me?" he asked again, ignoring her question. He pulled a chair out for her at the table and resumed his own place.

She said, "Remember when I kissed you in the restaurant?"

"I suppose so."

She grinned at him. "As I said, I was already smelling a rat, so I dropped my own I.D. tag into your jacket breast pocket. It was a calculated risk. I've noticed that men practically never put their hands into their breast pockets, possibly because they seldom carry anything there except a pen or handkerchief. So, when things had quieted down a bit, His Majesty got another fix on you. We thought it was a bit suspicious that you had disappeared from that cafeteria and the vicinity with so little difficulty. You didn't even shout for help. After the shock wore off, it was somewhat obvious that you had gone willingly, or possibly even on your own. So we got the fix on you, and here you are—way out in the boondocks in a cabin."

"Who's we?"

"The team, of course. We could have come and got you at any time we wished, but we wanted to figure out what you were up to first. That's what puzzled us."

She grinned at him again.

"And?"

"It was the Kike who came up with the answer. He used a process of elimination. It couldn't be the Americans who had you, because they were trying to work through me to get your secret. Nor Common Europe, since they were working through Brett-James. Nor China, since they had Li Ching. And not the Soviet Complex, since they were working through Max and Foucault. Who

else was in on the act, now that we had dispensed with the Mafia? The only answer was the World Government League.'' She paused for a moment. ''Which is currently, you'll be glad to learn, coming along marvelously,'' she added.

He shifted unhappily in his chair. ''Why should I be glad of that?''

''Because you are undoubtedly a member, darling, and undoubtedly very involved. And now so are all the members of the team. We're all behind you, darling—even Li Ching. It was all a fake, wasn't it?''

He looked at her for a long time. ''Yes, it was all a fake.''

''There never was an alien spaceship?''

''That's right.''

''The way we figured it,'' she said, ''was that one of your members of the World Government League, a top photographer, faked the pictures. It wouldn't have been very difficult to make an authentic-looking model spaceship, and dub in the moonscape background.''

''Yes, it was no big problem. He is one of the most accomplished photographers in the world.''

''One of your other members, a psychiatrist, I presume, planted an hypnotic something or other in your mind so that even under the truth serum you told the same story. That must have been a bit more complicated, but we discovered that it was not at all impossible.''

''That's right.''

''What are you planning to do now, darling?''

He sighed. ''The organization is hiding me out. We'll wait about a year, until this World Government thing really jells. Total international disarmament, united efforts against pollution and preservation of natural resources, complete cooperation in exploitation of solar energy, exploitation of the oceans and such, international cooperation in population control, so on and so forth. The World Government dream, in short."

"And then?"

"And then I'll come out of hiding and admit the hoax so that everybody can forget about an alien invasion."

For the first time, Mary Lou was aghast. "You fool, they'll lynch you."

"Probably. But by then we will have wound up with world government, which is the only solution to the mess we've gotten ourselves into."

It was her turn to sigh. "All right, I'll join you. The other members of the team won't show. Somebody might tail them and reveal your hiding place. We decided I would be the one to risk it now. A year, eh?" She looked about the cabin. "You're lucky I showed up. You certainly need a housekeeper."

He said huskily, "Not just yet. There's something I need more."

AFTERMATH

In his dramatic key speech before the Congress of the World Government, the Chairman began by saying, "Ladies and gentlemen of the world, no longer are we Caucasians or Blacks, Mongolians or Semites, Indians—of India or America—Eskimos or Malays, Australian Bushmen, or Congo Pygmies. No longer are we Swiss, Indonesians, Argentines, Zulus, Americans, or British. Ladiés and gentlemen of the world, united we stand . . ."

He wasn't able to complete his sentence. The applause lasted a quarter of an hour.

When it died down, he said, "We will now proceed to form the first World Government."